"Listen, it's a long story, but I have to warn you," I started.

Honey grabbed Dave's arm and asked again, "Who is this woman?"

"You want to know who I am?" I said, my voice rising in my throat. "I'm the woman whose place you took. I'm the woman who made the money for this trip possible. I'm the woman who should be standing next to Dave. This was my trip. Mine."

"What are you talking about?"

"I'm Dave's girlfriend." I refused to use the word *old* or *ex*. "Didn't he tell you about me?"

Dave's eyes shifted back and forth. I could see that he was still having trouble taking in the sight of the two sides of his life colliding. Pathetic man. I had to get out of there before I strangled him. "Look, the only reason I'm here—and I don't know why I bothered—is someone might be trying to kill you."

Dave shook his head. "Karen, I don't know what you're talking about and I don't want to know. . . ."

"If you don't believe me, ask *her*. . . ."

KILLER
LIBRARIAN

MARY LOU KIRWIN

POCKET BOOKS

New York   London   Toronto   Sydney   New Delhi

Pocket Books
A Division of Simon & Schuster, Inc.
1230 Avenue of the Americas
New York, NY 10020

This book is a work of fiction. Names, characters, places, and incidents either are products of the author's imagination or are used fictitiously. Any resemblance to actual events or locales or persons, living or dead, is entirely coincidental.

First Pocket Books paperback edition December 2012

POCKET and colophon are registered trademarks
of Simon & Schuster, Inc.

For information about special discounts for bulk purchases, please contact Simon & Schuster Special Sales at 1-866-506-1949 or business@simonandschuster.com.

The Simon & Schuster Speakers Bureau can bring authors to your live event. For more information or to book an event contact the Simon & Schuster Speakers Bureau at 1-866-248-3049 or visit our website at www.simonspeakers.com.

Designed by Davina Mock-Maniscalco

Manufactured in the United States of America

10   9   8   7   6   5   4   3

ISBN 978-1-4516-8464-3

ISBN 978-1-4516-8465-0 (ebook)

Merci mille fois to Janet

There are such beings in the world, perhaps one in a thousand, as the creature you and I should think perfection, where grade and spirit are united to worth, where the manners are equal to the heart and understanding: but such a person may not come in your way. . . .

—a letter to Fanny from Jane Austen

". . . how are you?" said Winnie-the-Pooh.
  Eeyore shook his head from side to side.
  "Not very how," he said. "I don't seem to have been at all how for a long time."

—*Winnie-the-Pooh*, A. A. Milne

"What are you thinking?" he inquired at last.
  I opened my mouth to reply, changed my mind and shrugged my shoulders. I could not bring myself to say it, but there was a dead body between us.

—*No Love Lost*, Margery Allingham

Acknowledgments

While I have visited England many times, I'm much more familiar with Sunshine Valley. For vetting the book in England I'd like to thank Janet Cox, Ida Swearingen, and Ellen Hawley. And for checking the book out, I'd like to thank librarian Mary Steinbicker.

Also, as always, my partner and critic extraordinaire, Pete Hautman. And my sidekicks: Pat Boenhardt, Deborah Woodworth, and Kathy Erickson.

Rosie, now there are two dead men."

"Karen, is that you?" a very sleepy voice asked me.

I knew it was the middle of the night in Minnesota, but I had to talk to someone. "This has not turned out to be the trip to England I thought it would be."

"Come home and we can talk about it," she said.

I could tell she was not even awake. Then she hung up the phone before I could explain.

How had I gotten to where I was?

ONE

Cracking the Spine

A week earlier

You know how it feels when you open the pages of a new book, the sense that all is possible, that this might be the book that will sweep you up so completely that you will lose yourself in its story, not stopping to eat or sleep or answer the phone, and when it ends, you will be close to weeping, knowing this experience might never happen again?

Well, that's how I felt the morning of my first-ever trip, with my boyfriend, Dave, to England, a place I had come to know intimately thus far only through books, starting with the Hundred Acre

Wood of Winnie-the-Pooh continuing to present-day London streets of Ian McEwan's *Atonement*.

A place of infinite promise and romance was how I viewed England. The thought that I would be there within the day made me feel as if bubbles were popping on the surface of my skin. Back to the homeland, for I'm of English descent: Nash, Karen Nash.

My trip, indeed, was to prove unforgettable.

Standing behind the counter at the Sunshine Valley Library, my assistant librarian, Rosie, was staring off into space and putting a couple more bobby pins in her short, spiky auburn hair, just for decoration. When she saw me, she wrinkled her nose and asked in her squeaky voice, "What are you still doing here?"

I shrugged, hoping that I didn't need to explain.

When she continued to stare at me with her big blue eyes, I said, "Just checking on things one last time. In case you needed anything from me . . ."

"I want you to get on that darn plane." She squinched her mouth to one side, "But as long as you're here, there is one thing I want to ask you."

Rosie was a good twenty years younger than me, but rather than the daughter I had never had, she was my best friend. She was slightly taller than me and weighed thirty pounds more than my 122 pounds—a little rounder than she wanted to be. I thought her absolutely gorgeous—lovely skin and fantastic dimples.

She had three tattoos, all birds and quite small, one pierced eyebrow, and a belly-button piercing, which I had never seen, thank the Lord. I finally got my ears pierced at her urging when I turned forty-five, but I wasn't quite ready for a tattoo.

While we both were library professionals, Rosie had made the transition to the twenty-first century as a media specialist; she was an absolute whiz on the computer. The title of plain old "librarian" still suited me.

Rosie was way into speculative fiction—often asking me her favorite question, *what if?*—and I was the champion of the mystery section. I loved the psychology of people pushed to the ultimate act of desperation and passion. I adored the classic hard-boiled guys—Raymond Chandler, Ross MacDonald, and Dashiell Hammett—but some of my favorite writers were the latest crop of British women—Frances Fyfield, Minette Walters, and our own Elizabeth George. The mysteries that asked the question *why?* were the ones I had always cherished.

Having read literally thousands of them, I was sure I knew every which way of killing someone.

I never thought a time would come when I would make use of it.

"Did I tell you that he came in again yesterday, the cute sci-fi guy?" Rosie whispered, her eyes wide with glee.

Rosie had developed a severe crush on a library patron. It happens. We librarians are only human. The young man she had her eye on came in about once a week. Rosie liked the kind of books he checked out: lots of sci-fi with a little gardening thrown in. She liked his glasses, thick black frames. And she liked his name: Richard Wrangler. The fact that he was a frequent library patron answered the first question we wondered about on seeing a cute man—does he read?

"You might have mentioned it two or three times," I said.

"How did you get Dave to ask you out?"

I thought back to when I had met Dave, who is a plumber, arriving at my doorstep with his box of tools. "I didn't really have to work very hard. It seemed as if it was meant to be."

"You make it sound easy. And now look, you're going to England together. What should I do to get this guy to notice me?"

"You could stop up your toilet."

When she gave me her slivered-eye look, I suggested, more reasonably, "You could comment on something he's taking out."

"What if I haven't read it?"

"Wouldn't be good to be caught in a lie so early on in your relationship. Maybe say something like you've heard it's a good book."

"I could do that." She fingered her eyebrow piercing. "Don't you think he's cute?"

I had only seen Richard once. He looked like I had always pictured Ichabod Crane, tall and thin to the point of it being slightly painful. "He's got a certain charm."

Rosie reached out and put her hand on my shoulder. "I can't believe you're leaving. I'm going to miss you. E-mail, snail mail, postcards are even good."

I nodded, getting a little misty. I couldn't believe I was going on this trip either, but I knew adventure was waiting for me over the ocean.

TWO

∽

What Now?

I was an efficient and organized packer. Of course I'd made a list of all I'd need, but the most important thing was figuring out what books to bring. I had been planning this trip for six months, saving books as they came along: Josephine Tey, Dorothy Sayers, even some Agatha Christie. Then came the winnowing them down to six, one for every two days of the trip. I knew they had books in England, but I just didn't want to be caught out.

I should say *we* had been planning this trip—Dave and I. Dave, the love of my midlife.

I'd been with other men. I was even married for two years and four months in my early twenties. Roger Lundgren had been my best friend in library school. When we both graduated it seemed natural that we should marry. However, when he realized that he liked boys better than girls, our parting was sad, but very civil. We had really enjoyed each other and had been such good companions. We still send each other Christmas cards.

After that I was wary with men. Plus, the opportunities did not present themselves very often—certainly not in my line of work. After all, most librarians are women: 84.6 percent, to be exact.

Dave and I met in our forties when he fixed my toilet. I was so happy to have found a man who could fix things—unlike the usual type I went out with, who didn't even know what a hammer looked like—that I felt we were meant to be together through the hardships of life. I ignored the fact that all he read was the business section of the paper and books on golfing—even though he didn't golf.

A year ago, Dave had been trying to design a new toilet. With the green movement coming on strong, he wanted to cash in on it. I suggested he figure out a way to create a holding tank where the effluence could be stored and flushed only once or twice a day, thus saving many gallons of water. I even gave him the name: the Flush Budget.

Dave patented the idea and sold it for a large chunk of change. He put my name on the patent and offered me half of the royalties, but I demurred. After all, I figured that soon our finances would be commingling. To celebrate, he suggested this trip to England.

When he told me he had bought airline tickets for London, I was so excited I snapped the pencil I was holding right in half.

I had the trip all planned out—what bed-and-breakfast we would stay at, what plays we would see, what museums we would visit. The one tour I had to strike off the list was a trip to Hay-on-Wye, a town in Wales with more bookstores than any other in the British Isles. Dave would have died of boredom.

Even though our plane wouldn't leave for hours, I was already dressed in my new outfit—a pair of beige knit pants and matching Eileen Fisher hoodie—bought especially for the trip.

As I primped in front of the mirror I took a good hard look at myself, cataloguing my attributes. Forty-six years old; five foot two; dark brown hair with a few threads of gray, cut in a stylish bob, blue

eyes, an okay figure. I needed reading glasses—a
badge of honor in my profession. One of my best
features was my feet, but I didn't often get to show
them off. I needed to lose twelve pounds and I
knew exactly which ones they were.

I had all my accoutrements for traveling set right
by the front door—the current issue of *Vogue* (always my little treat when I fly), the *New York Times*
tucked into my carry-on bag so I could do the cross-
word puzzle, oatmeal cookies, binoculars, and a few
choice books.

We had four and a half hours before our flight,
but I was ready to leave as soon as Dave arrived. All
I had to do was put on my lipstick.

I was picking out the perfect color when the
phone rang.

I checked caller ID. It was Dave.

Dave had not come over last night as he usually
did. It was my idea, really. I thought it would be
more romantic, build up the tension. He had been
busy for the past two nights, so we hadn't seen each
other for a few days.

"Hey, Dave," I said.

I had decided not to try out my British accent
on him yet. I wanted it to be a surprise. Like the
black negligee I had rolled up in my flannel nightgown and tucked deep into my suitcase. I had been

watching BBC television shows—"Are You Being Served?" and all the many versions of the Jane Austen novels produced by PBS—trying to perfect my accent.

"Yeah, listen, Karen."

"I can hardly believe we're really going," I said. "Can you believe it? I hope you're packed. Really, I could have helped you, Dave. Do you have your raincoat? When are you coming to get me? Let's leave on the early side."

"That's what I called about." He sounded all business. "I don't think this is going to work."

I felt my shoulders tighten, my throat turn to dust. But I managed to sound calm when I asked, "What isn't going to work? Is there something wrong with your car? We can take a cab. That might be easier."

"No, that isn't what I mean. I mean this whole thing."

"What whole thing?" My voice was rising. I couldn't help it. Tension did that to my vocal cords.

"Us. This trip," Dave answered.

"This trip! Now you're scaring me."

He cleared his throat. Not a good sign. He only did that when he had bad news to deliver. Like when he told me my burgundy 1950s-era toilet would have to be replaced. "Well, I've been thinking. I don't think we're right for each other."

I could hardly breathe, but I managed to spit out, "What are you trying to say?"

"Karen, you're great, but . . . it's over. It isn't anything you did. It's me."

"What about the trip?"

"That's what I'm trying to tell you, Karen. No trip. I've changed my mind. I can't go to England with you."

"But I have my passport."

"I know, but I think it's better this way."

"Dave?" I had to talk sense to him. The last time I'd seen him everything had been fine. He had loved my meatballs. Later, in bed, he had loved me.

He hung up.

"Dave?" I couldn't believe it. This simply could not be happening. I let go of the phone. It fell to the floor and lay there like a dead mouse.

I slid down onto the floor next to it. The walls of the room rushed in toward me and I had a hard time breathing.

Something broke inside of me.

That was the first time I thought of killing him.

I couldn't believe how fast my love, my deep abiding love for this man who had saved me from the emptiness of the middle of my life, could change into bottomless hate. I was a walking hate machine.

Hate, however, was a better feeling than the flood of despair that was pushing behind it.

What about *England*?

I had taken two weeks off from my job.

What would I tell Rosie and Nancy, the other librarian? And everyone else I had bragged to about this wonderful trip.

I was all packed.

Everything was in order.

Sitting on the floor, staring at the kitchen cabinets—angry beyond despair—I became very clear.

Nothing was going to stop me.

With or without him, I was going to England.

THREE

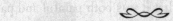

Mohammed Ali

After that first tsunami of hate washed over me, I tried to call Dave back. I'm not sure if I was calling him to berate him or to beg him to give me another chance.

No answer. I tried his home number, his cell number, I sent him an e-mail, I called his office. I left no messages until the second time I called his cell. He slept with his cell. I knew this because I had been in bed with both of them.

"Dave, we need to talk. If you're unhappy about some things, we could work them out on the trip.

I know I can be rather rigid, but I would like to change." I stayed calm, but by the word *trip* my mouth was quivering. I hung up before I cried.

What followed was a flood of tears, a tornado of wailing. I'd rather not go into too much detail here, but suffice it to say that it was both painful and pathetic. Afterward, I washed my face and reapplied my lipstick.

I stared at my watch. Our plane was leaving in three hours and thirty-three minutes. I was going to be on that plane if it killed me.

I called the airline and asked if there was any way I could get on that flight. That was the one thing I had Dave take care of—the plane tickets. "We've had some cancellations," the woman told me.

I tried to ignore the cost of a last-minute booking. How appropriate that I might be getting my own ticket back—at twice the price. I booked the flight, gave her my frequent-flier number, even though I was really an infrequent flier, and I was confirmed on the flight.

When the phone rang a few minutes later, I jumped for it so fast that I didn't even check caller ID. I was disappointed to hear Rosie's squeaky voice on the other end.

Her voice always reminded me of a mouse trying to talk like a human. "Karen, sorry to bother you, but that guy Richard came in again and returned his books and took out two others. He didn't use the speedy checkout, but brought them to me. Do you think that means something?"

"Possibly," I replied, not wanting to get her hopes up.

"I know you're leaving on your trip, but I didn't know who else to talk to."

"I am getting ready to leave." I hated to say my news out loud. Saying it to someone would make it all the more real. But I couldn't keep it from Rosie. "But not with Dave."

Stunned silence, then her thin voice yelped, "Oh, no. What happened? Is he okay? Did he have a heart attack?"

"No such luck." My voice cracked and I swallowed down tears. "He just broke up with me."

"What about the trip?"

"I'm going anyway."

"Wow, Karen, that's brave."

"I know." I tightened my top lip. I didn't feel brave. I felt a deep loneliness and wretched anger that the man who had been in my life for several years didn't have the guts to sit down face-to-face and tell me what was going on.

Even though I was the last person in the world who should have been giving advice to the lovelorn,

I wanted to help Rosie with Richard. I told her, "Maybe ask your guy a question."

"About what?"

"One of the books he's taking out."

"Yeah, I like that. I'll ask him if it's any good."

"But he won't have read it yet."

"That's right. I'll ask him why he's taking it out."

"Good plan."

"Dave wasn't good enough for you, Karen. I never liked his nose. Made him look like a toad."

"Thanks, Rosie." I had always liked his squat, turned-up nose. Not handsome, but neither was Dave. Because of that nose, I'd thought I could trust him.

I had to leave one thing behind. I opened my suitcase, unrolled my flannel nightie, and removed the black negligee. I wouldn't be wanting it now. I found a pair of scissors and was on the verge of slashing it to bits, when I thought again. Why rule it out? I do like to be ready for anything, and who knew what my future might bring? I folded it and put it back in the suitcase.

Cabdriver Mohammed Ali picked me up shortly before noon. He helped me put my one suitcase in the trunk. When I got into the backseat, I stared at his photograph and name, memorizing them just in case.

"Where are you going?" he asked.

"I'm going to England. My first time. I've never been before." I was babbling. Not a good sign. But if I talked I couldn't think about Dave, which would keep me from crying in the taxi.

"That's good, but I mean, what airline?"

"Oh." I told him.

"What time is your flight?"

I told him.

"You're plenty early," he said.

"I know. I don't like to rush."

"I lived in England," he said after we had pulled onto the freeway. "Before I come to America."

"Oh." I didn't feel much like hearing his life story.

"America's better. More room. Bigger cars."

"Yes, I suppose."

Halfway to the airport, Mohammed said, "Would you mind if I pull over for a few minutes?"

I wasn't really in a hurry. I assumed he needed to get gas. "No. That's fine."

He pulled off the freeway, turned onto a service road, and stopped on the shoulder. When he reached down under the seat, I started to worry. What was he doing? Was I getting kidnapped by a taxi driver? I touched my cell phone in my purse, in case I might want to use it.

As he surfaced from under the seat, I saw in his hands a rolled-up rug. He got out of the cab and put the rug down on the ground, facing east. Then he kneeled down on the rug and started praying. At least, I assumed he was praying.

When he got back in the cab, I asked him what he had prayed for.

"Always the same," he said. "To praise Allah and to ask him to take care of me and my family."

"Are you married?" I asked.

"Yes, I have four children."

"What would you think of a man who dated a woman for four years, made a huge pile of money, and then dumped her?"

"He will be punished."

His prophetic words calmed me. Dave would be punished.

With an hour to spare, I headed down to my gate, which was as far away as it could be from the entrance and still be in the airport. That was fine with me—I could use the walk.

I vacillated between being so angry with Dave that I wanted to tear his few remaining hairs out to feeling as if my heart had gone through a shredder and would never be mended again.

At the gate, I sat in the row of seats closest to the

windows and watched the airplanes take off. With every successful liftoff, I was relieved. I never quite understood how those big, heavy machines lumbered up into the air and managed to soar around the world.

I tried not to pay any attention to the couples around me, happy or otherwise—I couldn't bear it. If Dave were sitting next to me, he would be reading *USA Today* and complaining about something, but that was what I had loved about him. He didn't move easily through the world. Like a stolid tugboat, he created a wake.

I always use the bathroom right when they call the first-class passengers. Gives me a head start on the trip. Fifteen minutes before our flight was scheduled to board, I went into the bathroom.

After visiting the stall, I leaned in toward the mirror to see how red my eyes were. Not too bad.

I turned to exit the restroom, when a scrawny young woman with puffed-up lips and thin blond hair came whipping in. She was wearing one of the tightest T-shirts I had ever seen—the bones of her spine jutted through it—and jeans that hugged her knees and the bottom of her butt.

She almost ran right into me. "Sorry, I've got a plane to catch. Had to check on my makeup. Want to look good for my guy."

I heard a man's voice call after her, "Hurry, honey. I just heard them call our row."

I recognized the voice.

It was Dave's. He must have kept his ticket and bought a new one for this blond woman.

FOUR

Magic Pill

Crazy ideas of revenge raged through my mind—sticking her head down the toilet and depressing the handle a few times. My next thought was how I was going to get on the plane without Dave seeing and recognizing me.

I went back to the mirror and pulled out my sunglasses. That helped. Dave had never seen the outfit I was wearing. I had bought it special for the trip. I pulled the hood up. Now not even my mother would have recognized me.

"Honey" came flying out of the stall and stood at

the sink next to me. "Oh, I can't believe I'm going to England," she said.

"Neither can I," I said. At least we agreed on something.

"I'm not so sure about this guy I'm going with, but I figure what the heck, he can't be all bad."

"Want to bet?" I muttered.

She leaned in closer to the mirror and started to put on some lipstick. At least that shut her up for a second.

I turned on the water in my sink full blast, held my hands in the stream, and aimed. Water hit her full in the face and she gasped from the shock of it. Her straggly thin hair looked even thinner and darker wet.

I mumbled something that I hoped sounded like, "I'm sorry," then fled the bathroom, not quite believing what I'd done. After all, she had done nothing to me, except exist, and steal my man.

Dave was tapping his foot and pressing his lips together as I walked by him. He didn't like to be kept waiting. He didn't even give me a second glance.

I ran to get in line. My row had already been called.

When I got up to the stewardess, she asked me if I would mind being seated in first class, as a family had requested the seat I was sitting in. "We have a very full plane." She smiled.

First class. That suited me fine.

I was holding a glass of champagne in my hand and a copy of the *New York Times* in front of my face as Dave pulled a very bedraggled Honey behind him onto the plane. The cabin doors closed right behind them. Peeking out from behind the paper, I watched them as they lurched down to the coach section of the plane. I toasted the start of a very fine trip.

I took a huge gulp of my champagne as I faced another awful truth—and probably the main reason why I'd never been to Europe before—I was petrified of flying. Even though I knew it was a bad idea, I hadn't been able to stop myself from checking the airline statistics for the past year and found there had been a total of twenty-seven airplane crashes, in which eighty-seven people had died. Statistically I knew it didn't matter what had happened previously. When a plane takes to the sky, it's a brand-new roll of the dice.

I know my fear is unfounded. I know it's stupid. I know it makes no sense. It's ten times more dangerous to drive on the freeway than fly in an airplane. And nothing was going to keep me from flying to England.

In order to be prepared, I had memorized the Federal Aviation Administration's five-step survival plan:

1. *Count the rows between your seat and the exit.*
2. *Read the safety card.*
3. *Properly brace for landing.*
4. *"Stop, go, and stay low."*
5. *Get away from the crash site.*

I was only four rows from the front exit. I'm not sure what proper bracing is and the "stop, go" part of number four gives me trouble too. But getting away from the crash site would be no trouble for me.

I also have a magic pill I take. Unfortunately, this pill puts me to sleep, but since it would be a good seven hours before we landed in Heathrow, on this trip this side effect was a distinct advantage.

I took my pill with my second glass of bubbly and paged through my *Vogue* magazine. Many of the young models looked like Honey: no boobs, no butt, and probably no brain. Dave had turned fifty this last year. She had to be a good twenty years younger than he was. What was he thinking?

Before I drifted off to sleep, my eyes wandered out the window. Darkness was climbing up over the rim of the eastern horizon. I put my head close to the window and looked down. The earth, seen through billowing mattresses of clouds, appeared green and inviting.

Really I don't know what I was afraid of. Falling to death in an airplane would be quite a fantastic way to leave this world.

As I faded off to sleep, I thought maybe it wouldn't be so bad if the plane crashed.

At least then Dave would be dead.

FIVE

FIVE

❧

Mr. Toad

The stewardess gently shook my shoulder and said, "We're only an hour out. Can I get you something before we land?"

"Coffee," I managed to croak out. "Everything in it." I pulled myself up to a sitting position and first checked my watch—still early, only eight o'clock in the morning. Grey clouds swirled below me (note: grey, not gray). A gentle rain would be falling on the city streets, I was sure. Just the way I had always imagined London.

When I thought about Dave being on the plane,

anger threatened to swamp me. When I remembered he was with Honey, hate filled my mouth like bile. I wished he would fall off the face of the earth and drag his Honey with him.

Maybe it all would have turned out differently if Dave and Honey hadn't gotten their bags moments before me. We all got in line for the cabs at the same time. They were too busy smoochie-facing with each other to notice me standing a few people behind them. Who was this man? Dave had never liked to be intimate in public. With me.

I climbed into the cab right behind theirs and, without thinking, told the driver to "follow that cab." There I was in London—home of Sherlock Holmes, Jack the Ripper, the Woman in White—and I was following my ex-lover through the rainy streets of the capital city.

"What's up?" the cabbie asked.

"They forgot something on the plane," I replied, pleased with how quickly I had thought up a suitable lie. "This is my first time in England," I told the back of the cabbie's head.

He grunted, then said, "That's all right then."

Their cab dropped them off at a small, quaint hotel: the Queen's Arms Hotel. I pulled my hood up as my cabdriver slid in behind them.

"You going to get out?" the cabbie asked as I sat mesmerized, watching Dave and Honey. Holding hands.

That really galled me. Dave had never held hands with me. I had tried once or twice, but he shook me off quickly. I had always assumed it was not his style. But obviously, I was not the right woman. Probably not the right age.

"No, I just wanted to know where I could get hold of them," I said quickly.

Honey was in the lead, nearly dragging the now-named Mr. Toad down the sidewalk. Poor squat-nosed dear. It was about time for his morning nap, plus he was probably exhausted after the long plane flight. I was sure he hadn't gotten any rest on the flight with Honey talking his ear off, and those airplane seats could not have done his sciatica any good.

I gave the cabbie the address of the original B and B that I'd booked and tucked my head down farther into my hoodie, unable to watch anymore.

When my cab dropped me off in Hammersmith on Putney Street, I was disappointed with my first view of the neighborhood. After spending a few hours on Google Earth perusing this area, I had somehow seen it as quainter and more charming. Instead, I found myself in front of a whole row of identical gloomy, dark brick tenements that were all connected: The whole block was one long row house.

I found the address of my bed-and-breakfast, lifted up the large brass knocker in the shape of a hand, and let it clang down a few times. After a minute or so, the door pushed open.

A slight man only slightly taller than me with a ring of curly light brown hair around his head and sad but very deep brown eyes answered the door. His eyes lit up at the sight of me.

"Yes, may I help you?"

"Are you the bed-and-breakfast?" I asked.

The man looked me up and down, then answered, "I myself am not the bed-and-breakfast. However, I do own the bed-and-breakfast. I am Caldwell Perkins. Might I presume that you are Mrs. Nash?"

"Yes, I'm sorry. I am just Karen Nash."

"Why ever are you sorry about being Karen Nash?"

He stepped to one side and, as I walked by him, gently took my rolling suitcase from my hand.

"No, you know what I mean."

"I thought you were traveling with a partner, I assumed your husband?" he asked while he waved his hand down the hallway.

"You mean Dave?"

"I wasn't sure of the gentleman's name."

"Dave. Well, something came up. He couldn't make it." An image of Honey hauling him down the street, yakking, popped into my mind.

"That is disappointing."

Caldwell ushered me into the back room, the windows of which opened out onto an absolutely fabulous garden with—if I could believe my eyes— a fig tree. The outdoor space could not have been more than that of an average-size room, maybe twelve feet by twenty feet, but it looked like a perfect landscape, a pond right in the center of it, with roses and other blooming flowers, including penstemon, hollyhocks, and foxglove.

"Would you like to be shown to your room and then perhaps join me back here for a cup of tea?" Caldwell asked.

"That would be heavenly."

"We're having a touch of weather," he murmured as he walked me up the stairs, still carting my rolling bag.

"Yes, but rain is what I expected."

"Then you will not be disappointed."

"I've never been to England before, except in books. I've read so many English novels I feel like I know it already."

"My, your first time. We shall do all we can to make this a very pleasant visit for you."

I wondered if he was using the royal "we" or if he was married or perhaps had a male partner. Since my unfortunate marriage, I suspected most men of harboring secret desires for their own sex. Plus, it had to be said, he was a small, almost delicate, man who ran a B and B.

The landing at the top of the stairs was at the end of a hallway that had six doors off of it. We walked down to the far end, the farthest away from the street and overlooking, as I had hoped, the garden.

Caldwell opened the door to my room and I was pleasantly surprised. The room was simpler than I had thought it might be. Not floofy at all, but rather spare and elegant. The bed was high, with crisp white sheets; the curtains were white linen; and a dark maroon reading chair was tucked in a corner with a floor-to-ceiling bookshelf behind it, filled with books. A wondrous wall of books.

I couldn't help it. I let out a small peep.

"Is something wrong?" Caldwell asked.

"No, I'm just happy to see all the books," I explained. "It makes me feel at home." I resisted telling him I was a librarian. After all, I was on vacation and I could be anyone I wanted to be. Someone more adventurous.

"The tea is ready when you are."

"I'll be right there. Just give me a moment to freshen up." After Caldwell left, I ran some water in the bathroom sink and washed my face. Forty-six years old and I didn't look a day over forty-three. My short dark hair was curling a bit more than usual in this rainy weather, but I rather liked that look. A little softer.

I was as presentable as I could be at that moment, plus why did I care what I looked like? There was no one who knew me here. Except Caldwell.

"This is a beautiful room," I said as I walked into the sitting room. "You've got a lovely backyard."

"That is not a backyard. It is my back garden."

"Of course it's a garden. I remember that now. At home we call them backyards." I looked around the room and spotted an old glass-doored bookshelf filled with books all in cellophane covers.

Caldwell noticed my gaze. "Those are my first editions. Mainly British children's books, one of my specialties." Then he asked me, "Would you like some coffee?"

"No, actually I'd prefer tea."

He nodded. I thought I had pleased him. "Do you take sugar or lemon?"

"Just a touch of milk, please." I sank into a love seat, feeling the down cushions give way beneath me, and watched him pour the tea into a delicately flowered porcelain cup, put it on a wafer-thin saucer, and hand it me.

"So many Americans only drink coffee," he said, watching me with admiration.

"You get a lot of Americans?"

"I'm just about full up with them this week," he said. "Two retired ladies from Nebraska, Betty and Barb. They are rather hard to tell apart as they often dress alike. I think of them as the Tweedles."

"As in *Through the Looking-Glass*."

He nodded. "Exactly. Then there's an older gentleman with his new bride, Howard and Annette Worth, from Connecticut. They met when he was convalescing from a slight heart attack, not an unusual story, wealthy older man falls in love with his shy young nurse."

"I think I've read that story recently," I couldn't help but say.

He smiled and continued, "Both couples are here for a horticultural event, the Chelsea Flower Show. They come every year, although this is only the second year for Howard's new wife. I'm not sure she's into flowers. There's no love lost between the Tweedles and Annette. I think they're horridly disappointed that Howard married her. They always thought his first love was flowers."

"Oh, I'd like to hear about that show."

"Oh, you'll hear plenty. Then there'll be Francine, a French entrepreneur. Not at all interested in flowers. She sells lovely linens for a living. She's here on business." Caldwell paused and looked at me. "What do you plan to do while you are in London?"

"Find a good way to murder someone." The words pushed out on their own, surprising me with how calm I sounded as I said them.

Caldwell, bless his heart, didn't look too shocked. Instead he leaned back and tapped the tips of his fingers together. "How interesting. I'd love to hear more. Would you care to join me for a curry tonight and then on to a pub?"

"Jolly good," I said.

❧

SIX

Vindaloo Curry

Waiting in the front entry, Caldwell looked very British and quite dapper in a tweed jacket with a brown scarf tied around his neck. I felt a little more comfortable when I looked down and saw he was wearing jeans.

"How was your walk?" he asked.

I didn't want to confess that it wasn't much of a walk. I had managed to go all of three blocks, found a little tea shop, and plunked down and read a book, every once in a while glancing up to see if I was still really in England. "Fine. I'm starving."

"Do you like curries?"

"I love curries." The few times I had tasted them. I would have said I loved anything he had offered. I thought of Dave's reaction to Indian food the one time I had persuaded him to try it. He had taken a large mouthful of vindaloo and almost spat it out. "Are you sure you don't have anything else to do?" I asked Caldwell.

"It's my pleasure," he said calmly and helped me on with my brand-new, bought-for-the-trip, Burberry raincoat.

"Is this part of the deal?"

"I beg your pardon?" he said mildly.

"You know, part of the bed-and-breakfast deal. A single woman and you feel compelled to take her out? You know, entertain her?"

"Not at all. Many a woman I have let wander her way through the corridors of London on her own. I'm intrigued by your desire to murder someone, having been there myself, and wouldn't mind some company at the pub. Plus, I'm starving."

"I'm ravenous," I said. A curry sounded divine and very imperialistically English.

Just then a tall white-haired man and a small dark-haired woman burst through the front door, shaking rain off themselves and their umbrella.

"Cats and dogs," the man said. He was handsome

in a rather dissolute way, good posture, piercing blue eyes, but loose joints and a blowsy manner.

"A downpour," the small woman agreed. She would have been lovely had she not been so hunched over and scurrying. She had wonderful hair, but her eyes were small and looked down as if watching for mice.

Caldwell introduced us. "Karen, this is Howard and Annette Worth. They arrived yesterday. This is a new guest, Karen Nash, from America also. Sorry about the pouring rain."

"Good for the flowers, bad for the show," Howard muttered as he took off his raincoat and managed to shower us all with water.

Annette took the coat from him and hung it on the coatrack. Even though she was his wife, she was still acting as his aide. He strode past us all and then turned and asked, "Is there a fire going in the parlor?"

"Turn it on, if you wish," Caldwell said.

"Annette," Mr. Worth summoned, "please attend to that."

Annette peeled off her coat in a rush, then scooted past him down the hall.

"I'm off for dinner," Caldwell said.

Mr. Worth gave me a look as if I were a wilted flower specimen. "I see. Tomorrow's the big day. The show starts. We'll be up and out rather early."

"I'll have breakfast ready for you at six-thirty," Caldwell assured him.

"That should do." And without another word, Mr. Worth strode down the hall as if he owned the place.

The rain had eased up when we stepped outside. Caldwell had brought one big "brolly," as he called it. The two of us squeezed under it and walked the three blocks to his favorite Indian restaurant. He took my arm through his, I hoped a wonderful custom in England.

I fell in love with the restaurant as soon as we walked in. The smell of cumin and coriander hung thick in the air. Sitar music wafted through the room, as exotic as the smells. The walls were covered with red flocked wallpaper, which gave the place an odd elegance. The lights above the tables seemed at first to be made of the most intricate of metalwork, casting a delicate, perforated light on the walls, but when I looked at them more closely I saw that they were actually two colanders fastened together with a lightbulb in the middle. *How ingenious,* I thought.

"So, you like Indian food?" Caldwell asked, as we were seated by a thin, dark, and handsome man in a white shirt.

"I think so."

"You're not sure."

"The little I've eaten, I've liked. But I'm from Minnesota. We eat meat loaf and hot dish."

"Hot dish? What, might I ask, does that consist of?"

"That depends on what you have in the fridge— some form of starch, a smattering of meat, and almost always a can of mushroom soup. It's not haute cuisine, but rib-sticking good. We call it comfort food."

"Like Lancashire hot pot. Sounds very British." He opened up the menu. "Would you like me to order?"

"Yes, please," I said. "But let me have a look too."

Together we ordered twice as much as we could eat. I was starving and he was generous with our order. A chicken tikka, a lamb vindaloo, raita, dal, naan, lassi . . . Everything Caldwell ordered sounded good. Soon the waiter started bringing piles of food in small bowls of green sauce and red sauce and onions and nuts, then large plates of lamb swimming in a dark sauce, accompanied by mounds of rice.

We ate and talked a little. I had to eat a lot of rice to counteract the spiciness, but I loved the taste of it all.

Finally Caldwell pushed his plate back, looked at

me, and asked the very American question, "What do you do for a living?"

The word *librarian* pushed itself into the middle of my mouth, but I wouldn't let it come out. I was enjoying not being defined by my profession.

"Well, I'm slightly undercover," I said.

"My, that sounds interesting."

"But I guess I can tell you."

He leaned forward. "Let me guess."

"Really?"

"I'm getting quite good at this. Whenever I have guests, I try to suss out what their occupations are, and I'm often right on the mark."

"Okay, what do I do?"

"Someone who loves books, who's undercover, doing research, I presume. I'm guessing you're a writer."

I was immensely flattered. So pleased, in fact, that I didn't refute it. He was so proud of himself that I hated to dissuade him. Then words popped out of my mouth that surprised me. "You got it. I'm a writer."

He leaned back and nodded. "It's the way you look around. You seem to be studying everything."

"Really?" I asked.

"Yes. You have an air about you. How you notice things. The questions you ask. What do you write?"

I didn't have to think twice. There was only one kind of writer that I would ever want to be. "I write mysteries."

"Of course," he said, nodding his head. "Thus your need to find a way to murder someone."

"I'm doing research."

"Yes, I see."

"I'm working on a new mystery—it involves a crime of passion, a vengeful woman." I was continuing to be amazed by how easily these lies were coming to me. It was as if my life was a story and I was simply rewriting it.

"Tell me more."

My own life opened like a book. With the oddest sense of remove, I started to recount it to Caldwell. "This woman has been planning a trip to England for a long time with the man in her life, and on the eve of their departure, he tells her that he doesn't love her anymore, that he's seeing someone else. Of course the woman is brokenhearted, but quickly feelings of revenge overtake her and she decides to figure out a way to kill him that is so cunning that she won't get caught. She makes it look like the new girlfriend killed him. For his money." I stopped, surprised by where my imagination had taken me.

His eyes twinkled. "Sounds fascinating. So your

heroine is also the murderer? That's a different spin."

"I'm still working that all out. Not sure if she'll go through with it." I needed to change the subject. "Now it's my turn to ask questions. Do you run this bed-and-breakfast all by yourself?"

"Yes, my partner left me several years ago, ran off with someone. No warning and it was all dumped in my lap."

"You're kidding!"

"Why ever would I joke about a serious subject like that?" He smiled while he was saying this and I wondered if the smile was genuine. I didn't know him well enough to tell, but everything about him seemed honest.

"How awful. I know how you feel." I quickly took a sip of tea so no more words could come out of my mouth. I didn't want to talk about Dave. I asked the obvious next question. "Who was your partner?"

He laughed. "Oh, I guess I shouldn't use that word with you Americans. You think it means a homosexual arrangement. No, in my case, for better or for worse, and mostly worse, it was with a woman. The bad news is she left me the B and B, but the good news is she did really leave it to me—I am now unofficially the owner."

"You've done a nice job of keeping the place up."

"Thank you. I know the rooms aren't as grand as some people like—no swags, no chintz, no twee figurines—but that way it's easier to keep clean."

"Except for the books," I teased him.

The bill arrived and I tried to grab it, but Caldwell was quicker.

"Please let me treat you," I said.

"Not in a million years. I expect to learn a lot more about murder from you."

∽

SEVEN

Twad and Tweed

My first big mistake was not figuring out the way the Brits drink in a pub.

At the Cock and Bull we ran into some friends of Caldwell's, two older gentlemen, who introduced themselves as Twad and Tweed. They were both tall, with full heads of silver-gray hair. They occasionally watched cricket with Caldwell on Sunday afternoons. Within moments of greeting us, Tweed was taking orders for a round.

Caldwell suggested I might like to have a shandy instead of the beer.

"A shandy?" I asked. "Is that a kind of beer?"

"Beer and lemonade. Women tend to like it."

"Real lemonade?" I cringed.

Twad nudged Caldwell and said, "That's right. The Yanks call it Seven-Up."

"Worse yet," I said. "Plain beer sounds good to me. I'll have whatever you're having."

"Pints all around?" Tweed asked.

Again Caldwell tried to protect me. "How about a half-pint for you?"

"No, if everyone's having a pint, I will too."

The Indian food had been spicy and salty, and I found that I was terrifically thirsty. My pint came, looking more like a pitcher of dark beer to me, and I drank half of it very quickly.

"You like that then?" Twad asked.

"Like what when?" I said back.

"The ale?"

"Brilliant," I said, because I had been practicing saying *brilliant* all month long. I could say it with a pretty good accent, I thought, with a soft, slight roll to the *r*.

I wasn't the only one who had gulped the pint down in a quick hurry. Twad and Tweed weren't far behind. When we came to the bottoms of our glasses, Twad declared it was his round and went back up to the bar.

While he was gone, I took the time to glance

around the room, which was as I had always imagined an English pub being, except smaller and dingier. The ceiling was low and the room was dark, as if people had been smoking in it for a few centuries, which they probably had. The dark alcoves and odd nooks gave one the sense that intriguing conversations were taking place.

"How old is this pub?" I asked Caldwell.

"Fairly recent really, I'd say. Maybe early eighteen hundreds."

I nodded as if I drank in two-hundred-year-old pubs all the time. When Twad handed me my next pint, I proposed a toast. "To the old country and the new country, coming together."

We clanked our pints together and drank to amity across the waves.

"What brings you to London?" Twad asked me.

Caldwell raised his eyes slightly as he waited for me to answer.

"Doing some research," I said.

"You must go to the Victoria and Albert," Tweed effused.

"I was planning on it. I hear they have an excellent collection of swords." Which was true—I had heard that from a friend who did ironwork in his spare time when he wasn't cataloguing children's books at the Kerlan Collection.

"You're interested in swords?" Twad gave me a look and stretched his eyebrows up to the top of his head.

"As much as I'm interested in any weapons of destruction."

They all looked at me to see if I was serious. Caldwell gave out a hoot of a laugh and the two older gentlemen twittered along with him.

Twad said, "You Americans and your weapons of mass destruction. Liable to get us all killed."

We all laughed again.

I had never been much of a beer drinker, preferring a light chardonnay with dinner, but there was something about standing up in a pub with three English blokes that made the libation taste as good as any I had ever had. I had nearly finished my second pint without any trouble.

As Caldwell went off for the third round for all of us, Twad and Tweed started discussing a cricket game and I looked around the room.

A blond-haired man was standing next to me, nursing a glass of red wine by himself. While his face was somber, his eyes lit up when I turned his way. He nodded and said, "Cheers," lifting his wineglass.

I lifted my almost-empty pint glass. "Thanks. I

guess I should say cheers too. Or, as we say, here's mud in your eye."

"Why, you're an American," he said, and laughed. "I love your accent. I went to New York once. Great city."

"Yes, it is. But London is wonderful," I gushed, which was unlike me, but at the moment it felt wonderful.

"Can be sometimes," he murmured. "I'm Guy, by the way."

"I'm Karen. I just got here today—to London, I mean."

"On your own?" he asked.

With that question, what Dave had done to me came crashing down. "I wasn't supposed to be. A friend was going to come too, but then something came up. Actually, he called the day we were going to leave. And he told me he didn't want to be with me anymore. How could he do that?" What had gotten into me? Perhaps it was the ale making me speak so openly to a stranger.

"He did treat you badly," Guy said, with such gentleness in his voice that it took my breath away.

The thought of Dave's voice on the phone, telling me it was over between us, which I had been pushing into the far back reaches of my mind, came flooding forward, my feelings of grief and anger mixing together dangerously. The two pints of beer had unleashed the torrent.

I leaned forward and whispered, "Nothing has turned out how I expected—all because of Dave." I hated to say it out loud.

"What did he do?"

I took a deep breath. "We'd been going out for four years. He's a plumber with his own business. Does very well and now he's doing even better since I gave him the idea for a new kind of toilet."

"How does one make money with a toilet?" Guy asked.

"It's hard to explain, but toilets are like mousetraps: People are always looking for a better one," I said, not wanting to get into the scatological details. "Anyway, we've been planning this trip for over six months, I was so looking forward to it. I thought maybe even he might give me a ring and everything, and then, right as we are leaving, really, yesterday, he dumps me."

"That's a shame. And you such a nice woman."

"I think so. Most of the time." My head felt abuzz from the beer and the still very raw emotions.

He shook his head and looked straight into my eyes. "I know how you feel. Happened to me once, it did. Not a pleasant thing. And me ready to pop the question too."

"What did you do?"

He took my question seriously. "I went crazy for a while, thought of getting even in some horrible way, but in my line of work one has to be careful."

"Caldwell—he owns the B and B I'm staying at—I don't want him to know what happened with Dave. It's too embarrassing. It's nice to be able to talk to someone about it. You won't tell anyone, will you?"

"Of course not."

I asked, "What is your line of work?"

"Let's just say I do keep company from time to time with the seedier elements of this fair city."

"Oh." It felt like he didn't want to say any more about what he did.

Guy smiled and kept his eyes on me. "Is this awful man still back in the States?"

"Well, no, that's part of what's so awful. Dave—his name is Dave Richter—is here in London. We were supposed to come here together on the plane, but he broke up with me, and I came anyway, and he did too, on the same plane."

"Together?"

"No. He doesn't know I'm here." I had to take

a deep breath to say the next part, which hurt like below-freezing air rushing into my lungs. "And the worst thing—the worst thing of all . . . I still can't believe it." I didn't know if I could say it—it would make it more real.

"What?"

"He didn't come alone."

"Really?"

"He came with another woman."

"No." He said the word like a door slamming hard. "Of all the—"

"Yes, and she's half his age. He's fifty. I suppose some people would find her attractive, you know. She's got long blond hair and she's super thin. And she wears those shirts that don't cover your belly button. Not appropriate travel wear, I'd say."

"Right," he responded.

"Then . . . You're not going to believe this, but I followed them to their hotel. The Queen's Arms. What was I thinking? What if he had seen me?"

"We all go a bit bonkers at such a time. Go gentle on yourself." He nodded. "The Queen's Arms Hotel. Know the place. Not far from where I live. Bit gone to pot. Loos down the hall."

Not having a private bath would drive Dave wild. He didn't even like having me share his bathroom when I stayed over.

"So, if you had your way, what would you like to have happen to this bloke?" Guy asked.

Talking about it had made me feel better. "I don't know . . . something horrible, I suppose." I laughed. It came out sounding like a cackle. "You're not going to believe this, but I've actually been fantasizing about killing him."

Guy rolled his wineglass in his hands. "Very understandable. I've been there myself."

Just then Caldwell handed me my third pint of beer. "Good evening," he said to Guy. To me, he said, "Karen, we've commandeered a table on the other side of the room. When you're ready."

I swayed slightly as I stood there. I couldn't believe what I had just told this stranger. But it had felt good to get some of that anger off my chest. "I hope I haven't said too much."

"Not to worry," Guy said. "You'll be surprised. Dave will be taken care of. I'll make sure he is."

Caldwell took my arm as I started to walk. I was glad of his assistance. The floor of the old pub seemed to slant in all directions.

Twad and Tweed were sitting together on one side of the table. Caldwell and I slipped into the other side—a tight fit that forced Caldwell to keep an arm on the bench back behind me. The three men talked about cricket for a while, trying to explain the game to me, but I felt like Alice fallen down the rabbit hole. Or maybe Dorothy gone over the rainbow. Somehow I'd landed in a strange land in which I didn't know the rules.

"Wickets and crumpets and toppers," I mumbled. "Oh my."

Halfway through the third pint of beer I started to fade.

"I think it's time to call it a night," Caldwell suggested.

"But I haven't bought a round," I protested.

When I looked around, I saw that Guy was gone. No matter. Talking to him had done me good. I knew I would never kill Dave for real, but murdering him in my mind had helped a little.

EIGHT

Nodded Off

In the deep middle of the night I woke up. My head ached, my toes hurt, and everything in between was not feeling very good either. I didn't know where I was or what time it was, but I knew I needed to try to mend myself. I stumbled out of bed, crashing into the nightstand, then righted myself.

My head was trying to lift off my shoulders and go into orbit. I put both hands on it to keep it in place. Aspirin and orange juice might do the trick, might quell my body aches enough to get me back to sleep. I turned on the bedside light and squinted my eyes against the glare. My purse was by the door to my room, so I stumbled over there and found the bottle of aspirin I carried with me just in case of a sinus headache. However, I was well aware that what I was feeling was the result of too much drink on top of severe jet lag.

The clock read three in the morning. Everyone should be sound asleep. I could safely make my way down to the kitchen and see if I couldn't find some form of juice in the refrigerator.

Wrapping my bathrobe around me, I hoped I looked presentable enough if I ran into anyone. I opened the door as quietly as possible and stepped out into the hallway. A night-light shone on the floor so I could make my way without fear of running into anything or anyone. Down the stairs I went and turned toward the kitchen. There appeared to be a light left on in the sitting room, and I could see well enough to find a switch in the kitchen.

I found no orange juice in the refrigerator, but I did find elderberry syrup. It would have to do. The label said to mix with water. I found a glass and mixed the liquid half and half. Two aspirin and a large tumbler of some very sweet juice later, I thought I might live. But I didn't want to go back to my room quite yet. I decided to wander into the sitting room and look out the window until my head stopped swirling.

However, when I walked into the back room I found it was already occupied. Mr. Worth was stretched out in the most comfortable chair, his head tilted back, his eyes closed, his mouth a crack open.

He was a tall, lanky man who didn't quite fit into the chair, but slouched and sprawling, he managed. I put his age at about seventy, a spry seventy, although at the moment, his face looked awfully slack.

A book was cradled in his lap. I couldn't help but lean forward to see what it was. With its cellophane wrapper, it appeared to be one of Caldwell's prized first editions. I read the title—*Winnie-the-Pooh*. Seemed an odd choice for such a learned, older man, but maybe he found it amusing. I had always found the book completely hysterical.

I sat down opposite him on the love seat. I thought of waking him, but he seemed so peaceful and quiet that I decided to let him be. Plus, Caldwell had said he had a bad heart and it might startle him to have a strange woman wake him in the night.

But as my head cleared and I continued to watch him, a feeling grew in me that something was wrong.

Mr. Worth was much too peaceful, much too quiet. I stared at his chest and could detect no movement. But maybe he was a very shallow breather. Or maybe he had sleep apnea.

Then the thought struck me: Maybe he had sleep apnea and it was preventing him from breathing at all. I forced myself to walk up very close to him. Looking down, I noticed that he was holding the book upside down. I slipped it out of his hands, closed it, and reshelved it in its proper place.

When I could still see no movement in Howard, I put out my hand and touched his neck. Neither warm nor cold. I could detect no pulse, but I wasn't really sure where to feel for it.

When I took my hand away from his neck, he fell forward. His chin hit the edge of the chair and then his head turned, somehow landing crooked in his own lap. Not a natural position at all.

I shrieked. The elderberry syrup threatened to come back up. My breath came in gasps.

A hand tumbled free and hit the floor and I shrieked again.

Swallowing another scream, I managed to say, "Mr. Worth?"

But I knew I was talking to a dead man.

NINE

Dial 999

Three doors banged open almost simultaneously. A thunder of footsteps hit the hallway upstairs, then came pounding down the stairs.

I stepped back from Howard Worth. Caldwell stopped in the doorway and looked at me.

"You screamed?" he asked.

I pointed at Howard, slouched over in his chair.

Two older women in matching plaid bathrobes pushed past and stood right in front of Howard. I guessed they were the Tweedles.

One of them asked, "Is he all right?"

The other said, "He doesn't look all right."

Then, as Caldwell came forward, Annette appeared behind him, wrapped in a pink chenille robe and shivering.

"What's going on?" she asked in a high, thin voice. "What's Howard doing sitting like that?"

Caldwell pushed between the Tweedles and knelt down in front of Howard. He checked his pulse in a couple places. He pushed the lifeless man back so he was sitting upright in the chair. Turning to me, he said, "Call emergency. It's nine-nine-nine. I think he's gone, but we need to try."

As Caldwell held Howard up in the chair, I pulled out my cell, but realized it would be a long-distance number and I'd never manage it. Then I grabbed the phone that was on a small table by the fireplace and dialed the number.

As I gave the woman who answered the information, I watched a small tableau form in the room. Annette crumpled at Howard's feet; Caldwell half knelt, pumping at Howard's chest; the Tweedles stood behind Annette, like two bookends leaning into each other for support.

Time slowed and eddied around us. Caldwell finally propped Howard with a pillow and stood up. Annette was sniffling and leaning on Howard's knee. The Tweedles sat down on the love seat and bent their faces into their hands. I stood by the doorway, ready to let anyone in if they would only come and knock.

About the time I had started to shred my bathrobe belt with nervousness, there was a pounding at the door and I let in three large firemen and a medic. They took over the room, pushing Caldwell out into the hall. The Tweedles retreated to the stairs, and Annette stayed huddled in a corner of the room, watching.

The medic, who looked like he had barely graduated from high school, tried to get a pulse—or a nonpulse, as the case might be—poked and prodded Worth, opened his eyes, shone a light on them, then dropped his hands and stood up.

"How long has he been like this?" the medic asked.

I answered, since I was the one who'd found him. "It's been at least ten minutes. But I found him this way, so I have no idea how long."

"He's dead," the medic said and snapped his bag shut. "I'll call it at three-fifteen."

TEN

The Morning After

The next morning, I found Caldwell tucked behind the *Guardian* at the small table in the kitchen, with an empty cup and saucer sitting in front of him. He looked like he had been up for a few hours and like his head wasn't pounding at all.

He gave me a grim smile. "You had a long night. They took Mr. Worth's body away very shortly after you went back to bed. Unfortunately, his death was not unexpected. His wife should probably not have let him come on this type of trip. His heart, you know. It's not been in good shape for a while. But it's still very sad." Then he said, "No one else is up yet. Are you ready for your tea?"

"Gallons, please. I'm still fighting off jet lag." He stood up and shooed me out of the kitchen. A few minutes later, he came into the sitting room with a silver pot and poured me a stream of tea.

"Jet lag can be nasty," he concurred.

"And three pints of beer didn't help either," I reminded him. "Which is about six times what I normally drink."

"Oww, I wondered," he said. "I forget that you Americans aren't used to the real stuff."

He was trying to tease me, and I was hardly in the mood. "Of course, I suppose it didn't help that Thad and Treat kept ordering more rounds."

"Thad and Treat?" I asked, wondering who he meant.

"You know, the two old chaps who joined us last night."

I almost laughed. "I thought their names were Twad and Tweed." I had to hold on to the sides of my head, as any movement was causing it to throb.

"They really are nice old fellows. It's hard to find people to talk cricket with these days."

"I suppose, what with the sticky wickets and all."

Caldwell laughed, then said, "I'll go get your breakfast."

As he went back down the hall, I vaguely remembered him asking if I would like a real English breakfast in the morning. Not knowing what else to say, I had agreed to it. Usually I had peanut butter on toast for breakfast.

He came back carrying aloft a large plate, which he plunked down in front of me with great ceremony. My eyes widened and my stomach shivered. There were two eggs swimming in grease, with four sausages nestled next to them, and a piece of bacon with a grilled half tomato. Thank goodness for the bread cooling on a rack next to the plate.

"You *are* going to eat some of this, aren't you?" I asked.

"No, that's all for you. I don't usually eat much for breakfast."

I knew the eggs would be good for me and I thought I could probably stomach the tomato. I wanted to tip the plate and pour off all of the grease, or at least pat it with my napkin, but I knew that would not be the thing to do. I held up one of the eggs on a fork and let it drip a bit before I carefully placed it in the middle of a piece of toast. When I took a bite, it tasted better than I expected. I found I was somewhat hungry.

Caldwell asked, "I'm sorry about your first night in England. But I suppose you could use it for research."

For a moment I had no idea what he was talking about. Then I remembered that I was a mystery writer. "Well, before finding Mr. Worth, it went fine. When you went up to the bar, I talked to some blond guy there who said he hung out with the seedier elements of London. He said his name was Guy. I never quite figured out what he does though. Maybe he's a con man or something. Do you know who I mean?"

"I have seen him in the pub before, enough to say hello. I do think I had heard that he hung out with a rough crowd. Being as calm and mild mannered as I am, I don't tend to hang around those sorts."

"Of course," I said.

"What's on your schedule?" he asked.

I thought of the long itinerary I had printed out for Dave and me: the museums, the shops, the teas, the gardens. Some of it I would still do, but the stuffing was coming out of me, and I wasn't sure I wanted to fill myself up with all that culture. I had finished my one egg sandwich and had done a pretty good job of dissecting the tomato, but the sausages I was avoiding.

"I'm not sure."

"Oh, really." Caldwell looked at me in surprise. "I imagined you with a long list of things to do. I had you down as a planner."

"Usually I am. But—" I really didn't want to explain about Mr. Toad, so I used Howard Worth's death. "A death like that really changes the way you look at everything. I'm not sure what I'm going to do today."

"Yes, I know what you mean. You feel like you need to make sure you're not wasting time."

"Or if you're wasting time, you're enjoying doing it. I think I'll go for a walk."

"That always gets me thinking, but it's raining again." He nodded toward the drizzling outdoors.

"I bought brand-new pull-on rubbers for the trip, and I have an umbrella. I'll be fine. I'll go for a long walk, then maybe come back and sink into the couch and read. If that's okay?"

"That's what the sofa is here for." He offered me a titch more tea. "Did you bring any work with you?"

Again I had to remind myself that I had claimed I was a mystery writer. I was all ready to come clean about my life, when he smiled and said, "I feel honored having you stay with me—a real writer and all."

I couldn't confess, what with him being so impressed by who I wasn't.

"Are you going to do some more research on ways to murder someone today?" he asked with a charming smile. "Any chance you'll try to visit Scotland Yard? The Tower of London?"

"Perhaps." The tea was hitting my system, and I was feeling very much more myself, ready to have a conversation, and I knew just what I wanted to talk about. "But as I recall, you said something about once wanting to kill someone yourself. How so?"

"I'll tell you someday," he assured me.

"Sounds like a good story."

"Aren't they all, when they're our own?"

"If you would care to talk about it now, it might help me with my research. I'm really trying to understand the psychology of such a desire for revenge. What would someone have to do to one to make one want to kill them?"

Caldwell tucked his chin and looked at my plate. I couldn't tell if he was thinking about what I was asking him or trying to avoid the question all together.

After a moment, he lifted his head up, smiled and said, "Run off with your best friend."

"I'm sorry." At least Mr. Toad had picked someone I'd never met.

"You don't have to finish all that food. I know it's a bit much. But I thought you should know what a real English grill was like."

Just then Annette slogged into the sitting room.

She looked like she hadn't slept at all and that instead she had cried. My heart went out to her.

She had dark brown hair pulled into a sloppy ponytail at her neck and was wearing a chenille bathrobe over what appeared to be an old T-shirt and flannel pajama bottoms. Her long face was pale as snow, but, unlike the fairy-tale princesses, she had red eyes instead of red lips. Her lips were nearly the color of her skin and she seemed to be chewing on them.

Caldwell hopped up. "Annette, you're up so soon?"

"The sedative put me to sleep, but it didn't keep me there." She hunkered down on the love seat, looking like she was going to try to take a nap. "I can't believe what's happened. It's like the worst dream in the world and it's happening to me and I can't wake up from it."

"I'm so sorry," I murmured.

She looked at me. "You're the one who found Howard, right? How did he seem? Peaceful?"

"Very."

"I tried to make him come to bed, but he insisted on another cup of his noxious tea and a little read. He never sleeps much. I was going to try to come down and get him, but I was exhausted and fell right to sleep. I should have insisted he come to bed." A grimace passed over her face; then she cried, "It's all my fault."

I have to admit I jumped to the conclusion that she was confessing something to us, but Caldwell saw it otherwise.

"I doubt anything could have prevented his heart attack. It was inevitable," Caldwell said.

"That's what they all say once it's happened. But Howard was doing so well. I had him on a really good regime and he was feeling so much better. I would never have let him come on this trip if I thought it would be too much for him. I was sure he'd live a good many more years. He deserved better." She collapsed on the couch, her head tucked into her arms, and sobbed.

"Well, the autopsy will give you some answers," Caldwell assured her.

"Oh, I wish they didn't have to do an autopsy," Annette said. "Howard would not have wanted to be dissected like one of his plants."

"However, in cases like this, it's usual . . ." Caldwell started to say and then thought better of it. "I'll get some tea." He left me in the room with a sobbing woman I didn't even know.

I, too, wondered why Annette would not want an autopsy, but I knew some people were squeamish about such things. I've never been that good with sympathy, but I figured I'd better try with Annette. I went over and patted her on the back. In a way, we had something in common—we had both lost our men. After quite a few pats, she finally sat up again, wiping her face.

I knew I should say something. "Did your husband love Winnie-the-Pooh?"

Annette looked at me as if I was some crazy old lady. "No, he hated that dopey bear. Called him Whiney the Poop. Why?"

"Oh, I just wondered." Strange that he'd ended his life reading about the bear. This bothered me.

I went back and curled into my chair and felt like I was one of the characters in *Winnie-the-Pooh*.

How I wished I was Pooh himself, with his immeasurable optimism, but at the moment I was more like Eeyore. With my sad tail dragging behind me as I sat, not knowing what to say, I couldn't help wondering what I was doing all by myself in this melancholy country.

ELEVEN

Biting Dogs

He was to get an award, and now I'll have to get it for him. I hate that kind of thing," Annette said. "No one knows this, but I hate flowers."

I wasn't quite sure what to say to this revelation. "Not everyone has to like flowers," I tried.

"Howard thought they did. He spent more time on his roses than he ever spent with me."

Annette said no more and I excused myself and went to my room. I knew that anger was one of the steps of grieving, but I hadn't realized it could come

so soon after a death. Annette had sounded posi-
tively mad at Howard. How strange.

I needed to get out of the B and B. Because of
the rain, it would be a good day to go to the National Gallery, one of the many museums on my list.

While I wasn't crazy about ships or trains, I
wanted to see my favorite painting by Turner: *Rain,
Steam and Speed*. I loved what he did with the ve-
hicles, how weather and emotion swirled around
them in his work. I had been looking forward to taking Dave to see it. I'd thought the trains and boats
might grab his attention.

The museum was open until six, which would
give me plenty of time to wander and have tea in
their café, which had a very good reputation. Funny
how the thought of tasty pastries and tea could
cheer me up. I patted at my hair, swabbed some lipstick on my face, and set out to brave the London
transportation system.

I took only two wrong turns in finding the tube,
as they call it; then I couldn't quite figure out how
to work the machines to get my tickets. A sweet
woman helped me, even though I didn't understand
a word she said. I could have sworn she was saying
something about an oyster card. So much for my
work on the British accent.

As I seated myself in the car, I couldn't help

being excited about riding in the tube, surrounded by people of all skin types and hair configurations. I knew I must look quite odd to them in my royal blue raincoat with my short bobbed hair. I wondered if they could tell I was a librarian from America—or if they might possibly think I was a mystery writer.

When we were let out at the Charing Cross stop, I emerged from the underground right in front of a huge stone building on Trafalgar Square. I had to remind myself several times which way to look as I crossed the streets. No wonder the Brits literally wrote on the street, right next to the curb, *look right,* so those backward Americans wouldn't get hit by a vehicle.

I forced myself to skip the bookstore and gift shop. The bookstore was usually where I started a tour of a museum. It drove Dave crazy that I wanted to see what I was going to see before I saw it.

The feel of the Gallery was distinctively different from that of an American museum—the rooms were somewhat small, much more filled with paintings than at home, and the walls were dark—which made it feel more like I was wandering through an art lover's home rather than a museum. As I stepped through each room, I felt a deep intimacy with the works of art.

I walked from room to room, letting a painting

I could see through an archway pull me on. Many Madonnas gazed down from the walls—wide-faced Belgian Madonnas; sallow, long-faced Spaniard Madonnas; even the small and lovely *Madonna of the Pinks* by Raphael.

But what struck me again and again as I wandered from room to room were the dogs. They were usually tucked into the corner of a painting, under the edge of their master's robes. They were what I would call curs. Small, odd, no-breed dogs that looked stocky and tough. You had a sense that if they decided to grab onto your ankle and shake, you might be in serious trouble.

Finally, I could wait no longer and took myself directly to the room that housed the Turners. The paintings were much smaller than I'd thought they would be. In reproductions, they seemed magnificently large. My second surprise was that this in no way diminished their power.

My third and most surprising surprise was that standing in front of the one painting I most wanted to see, *Rain, Steam and Speed,* was the one person in the whole wide world I did not want to see.

Yes, Dave the plumber had somehow managed to ferret out my favorite painting and was standing staring at it. It shouldn't have surprised me so much. I had talked about it quite a bit as we were planning our trip. I just hadn't thought he was listening to me.

I was rooted in the doorway to the room, hoping that he wouldn't turn and see me, but stapled to the spot. He was standing where I should be.

In that moment I saw Dave as if he was someone else's boyfriend (which he was), a schlumpy American in a sodden beige raincoat, the little remaining hair he had plastered to his glistening pate. His posture was slumped—belly forward, shoulders down, chest concave. He was no prize.

I had the overwhelming urge to run at him and push him in front of Turner's speeding locomotive, but I controlled myself and stepped back around the corner into the previous room.

As I leaned against the wall, my head was spinning. What did it mean that he was looking at my favorite painting? Was he still thinking about me? Where was his Honey? I wanted to make like the Wicked Witch of the West and melt away.

I happened to glance across the room at a large painting of a dolled-up man in a ruffled collar and his snarling dog. The dog looked so vibrant I believed it could have jumped out of the gilded frame.

In that moment I decided I would become that dog, that happy, snappy dog. I would stand my ground, wherever that happened to be.

Pushing off the wall, I turned back to the Turner room, just in time to see Dave shake his balding head at my favorite painting and walk off, disappearing through the opposite doorway. I waited a few beats to make sure he was really gone, then walked over to the Turner painting and planted myself right in front of it, ready to claim it as my own.

The locomotive was steaming toward me in diaphanous and glistening light.

TWELVE

Clotted Cream

The National Café was enormous—cheery and clattery. The waitstaff bustled around and people came and went with a sort of flair. A soft fog of light drifted in from the floor-to-ceiling windows.

I asked to be seated way in the back, near one of the tall windows, out of the way so I could hide behind a menu if I saw Dave or Honey coming in.

After glancing out at the drizzling rain, I gave myself over to watching the people around me: women in flowing red and gold saris, men in tweed jackets, girls with pierced eyebrows, and red-cheeked boys in school uniforms. I kept reminding myself that I was one of them: I was now a world traveler.

I pored over the menu, wondering what I should have, knowing full well that it was the afternoon tea I would splurge on, with its finger sandwiches and its clotted cream, but I considered fish and chips and even some oddly named desserts like Eton mess and treacle tart.

The waitress came, a whip of a girl with dark black hair spiking out from a topknot on her head, and asked, "Wha'jou like?"

I said, "The full cream tea, please," in my most perfected English accent and she did a double take.

"Cor, I could have sworn you were an American and you'd want a hamburger."

I just dipped my head, not wanting to risk saying another word. When she scurried away, I had to give a little laugh. Maybe I did belong here after all.

Even though I hated people who did this, I decided that since I was off in a corner by myself, I would call Rosie on my cell phone. I was wondering how she was doing without me, but also, I needed to talk to someone I knew.

Since it was five in the afternoon here, it would be eleven in the morning in Minnesota and she would be at work. I dialed.

Rosie answered, "Sunshine Valley Library. How can I help you?"

"Hey, Rosie."

She squealed when she heard my voice. It wasn't hard to make her squeal, but I was glad to hear the sound just the same.

"Where are you?" she asked.

"London, England."

She squealed again.

"Specifically," I went on, "having tea in the National Gallery café. I've been wandering through the museum."

"How I'd love to be there," she whispered. "How's it going? Did you get jet lag? Are you doing okay— by yourself and everything, I mean?"

"I guess I'm fine. It's been a weird day. I found a dead man at the B and B last night. It's assumed he died of natural causes and all, but I'm not sure, and it's still very unsettling, and then I almost ran into Dave in this museum. Oh, I didn't tell you—he and his new girlfriend were on the same plane as me. I feel jinxed."

"Wow. You *are* having adventures, aren't you? How did the dead man die?"

"He was older, in his seventies, and I guess his heart gave out. But he was holding a book upside down and for some reason that has me thinking there might be more to his death than meets the eye."

"You do love your mysteries," she said, then asked, "What would you have said to Dave?"

"I'm not sure I would have said a thing. I feel like he doesn't belong here. This is my country. I'm claiming it for my own."

"Good for you."

"Oh, the one good thing. I went out with a fellow to a pub last night."

"You went out with a fellow? My, aren't you the fast worker? What's he like? Don't you just love a British accent?"

"No, it wasn't like that. It was only Caldwell, the man who runs the bed-and-breakfast I'm staying at. I had fun, but I also had a little too much to drink. Actually, I had gallons too much to drink."

"Even better. Is he cute?"

I thought about Caldwell. "Yes, I'd say he's cute. But better than that, he has a lot of books. If I had known, I wouldn't have had to bring any." I oddly felt uncomfortable talking about Caldwell. "How's it going with your sci-fi guy?"

"Oh, you're not going to believe it. I actually talked to him. He took out one of my favorite books. An Ursula Le Guin. I mean, I had to say something. And it came out very naturally. He seemed interested in what I thought about the book. He even asked me questions about what else I liked. I told him I would give him a list. I've been working on it all morning."

"Try not to make it too long, Rosie. You don't have to train him in all at once."

"Yeah, I guess you're right. But I want it to be good. I want the list to show him who I really am."

"I understand." I saw the waitress approaching with my tea. "Listen, I have to scoot. Food is appearing. How's everything going at the library?"

"Everything's fine. Listen, Karen, avoid dead men and deader ex-boyfriends. And don't worry about the library. We hardly miss you."

Not what I wanted to hear. I was surprised by how much I missed work, wandering around the library, knowing my place in the world. I wished her luck with Richard, said good-bye, and snapped my cell phone shut.

The waitress put down the teapot first and reminded me to let it steep a few more minutes. Very civilized. She set down two platefuls of scrumptious food: elongated sandwiches of pure white bread with slivers of cucumber tucked in between, perfectly browned mounds of scones. I took my time, looking over the gorgeous plate of food, forcing myself to eat it slowly. Like a good girl, I ate my sandwiches first, then gave myself into the melting sweetness of the scones and cream and jam.

I couldn't get over the fact that I had just seen Dave, much as I wanted to rip him out of my mind. I remembered the first time I met him. He was recently divorced and I had taken a year off of dating after a long-term affair had run out of steam. Then came the disaster that brought us together.

One evening as I was getting ready for bed, the toilet started running. The next thing I knew it was overflowing. But this wasn't a slow dribble. That could have waited until morning. A waterfall erupted, flowing all over the whole bathroom and out into the hall. It had to be stopped. I called an all-hours plumber and Dave happened to be on call that night. Minutes later he was at my door, tools in hand.

Nothing like being rescued in the middle of the night to make a woman's heart grow very fond. He fixed the faucet with a few quick turns of his wrench and I offered him coffee. We talked for a while until he got his next call. I was sorry to see him go.

Two days later Dave called and asked me out.

After seeing him in the Gallery, I couldn't help continuing to wonder where his new girlfriend was and why he had been checking out my favorite painting. I imagined running into him as I left the National Gallery. Him standing droopily in the rain, seeing me and breaking into a big smile.

"I've been waiting for you," he would say. "I hoped you would be here. That's why I came."

I would look down my nose at him and say, "Do I know you?"

"Would you like more hot water for your tea?" the waitress held out a large teapot.

I jumped, then smiled up at her. Just in time, I remembered my accent. "Ta, that would be lovely."

Dave was completely out of my life. All I had to do was remember for a fraction of a second what it had felt like to get his phone call telling me we were done. After all our time together, he couldn't even tell me face-to-face. And I had thought him brave. The bolt of pain, anger, and, yes, devastation that cracked through me was enough to warn me off any thought of even talking to him again. Even if he came begging, crawling on bloody stumps to me, I would not have anything to do with him again. Once a man has dumped you like that, there is no going back.

Looking out the big windows, I could see that the sky had lightened and the rain was only spattering. Maybe tomorrow would be bright and sunny. A good day to take a long walk, maybe even go to a garden.

I paid my bill, walked out of the museum, and stood for a few moments on the stone steps, taking in the scene and looking forward to my tube ride home.

Off to my left down at the bottom of the stone stairs, I saw a young woman fling her shoulder-length hair back from her face and pull out a cigarette. She had one of those perfect bodies, tall and lanky, that all clothes looked good on. An equally tall blond-haired man was hovering about her.

I looked more closely, hoping to see a bit of English-style romance in action.

But as I stared, I saw the young woman was none other than Honey. Figured she'd be out here, rather than inside looking at the art. The blond-haired man leaned over and lit her cigarette.

I couldn't see his face, but his physique looked familiar. Too thin and too much hair to be Dave, and too tall to be Caldwell, and who else did I know in London?

As the man pivoted and sauntered off, I got a glance at his face. Guy, the man I'd spilled my heart to in the pub. What was he doing here? I ran down the steps and tried to follow him.

I raced toward him, but the light had changed by the time I reached the street. The traffic came from either direction like a river charging wildly about.

I would not have dreamed of trying to run through that sea of cars and busses, no matter what direction I was told to look.

Guy turned when he was half a block away and saw me. I was pretty sure he saw me. He smiled and held his hand up. He pointed his finger up in the air, made his hand like a gun, and acted as if he was shooting at Honey.

Then he turned and was lost in the crowd.

THIRTEEN

Barb and Betty

When I let myself into Caldwell's, the house was quiet. Like a morgue, I thought, and then squelched that thought.

I walked up to my room, wondering how and why Guy had been talking to Honey.

His appearance on the steps of the National Gallery couldn't be a coincidence. Such enormous stretches of serendipity only happened in books, and usually in not very good ones. I think what worried me most of all was the gesture he had made with his hand of shooting at Honey. What had I set in motion?

From the silence in the house, I deduced that Caldwell was not home, which was fine with me. I couldn't talk to him about what had happened and I didn't think I was capable of talking about anything else. I wasn't hungry after my large and delectable tea. The evening stretched ahead of me, my second night in London, but I didn't want to go out again. I wanted comfort.

A bath and a book. That was what I wanted. The perfect combination of my drugs of choice.

I went to my room and started a tub, then, while I was waiting for it to fill, perused Caldwell's library. I had always felt that you could learn so much about a man by what he read. I should have been forewarned when I had seen a puny pile of Dean Koontzes and Robert Ludlums next to Dave's toilet.

Caldwell, on the other hand, had exquisite taste: from Philip Larkin to Gerard Manley Hopkins, from Jane Austen to Henry James. But he was not a total literary snot. Tucked in its proper place was a small stash of Dick Francises and the complete oeuvre of John le Carré.

What would be the perfect book for this moment?

I really wanted to read in the tub and I didn't dare do that with one of Caldwell's books so I had to select one I had brought along. I decided on a Josephine Tey. She was quintessential English, old-school, not too gory. A trip to the past would be the thing to help me forget my worries.

I sank into the tub carefully, holding the book up high, then equally sank into *Tiger in the Smoke*. I had read it many years ago but had forgotten most of it. The atmosphere was foggy London, and I read until the bath turned cool and my skin was a maze of puckers.

The water drained out of the tub with a gurgle as I toweled off. In this quiet moment, I took in deeply for the first time that I was in England, in London, away from my life. I could be someone completely different.

I *was* someone completely different: I was a mystery writer doing research, I was a scorned woman who had railed against her old lover to a stranger in a pub, I was a world traveler who ate scones in the National Gallery.

But looking down at my sturdy but curvy body, I was still me. I hurt from Dave's rejection, yet I was energized from my day in London. I was scared about having run into Guy again, by how one could set something in motion and not know how it was going to end. Having just seen a dead body, I knew how bad things could turn out.

I felt awful about the death of Howard Worth, but more than anything, I was puzzled by it. Something seemed wrong and out of place about it. How could I even say this—but I didn't think his death was an accident.

I pushed that thought out of my mind. I was not a mystery writer, no matter what Caldwell thought. I was a tired librarian, ready to crawl into bed with a good book by a master storyteller.

Then I heard wailing coming from right beneath me, like an Irish banshee foreshadowing a death. Or mourning a death.

I tied on my new, purchased-for-the-trip, pink flannel bathrobe, checked myself for a moment in the mirror, slipped my feet into a pair of darling satin slippers also bought for the trip, and set off downstairs.

A trio was ensconced in the sitting room—the two broad-boned women I had seen in the middle of the night were crammed into the love seat and Caldwell was across the room in his high-backed chair. He stood up to greet me.

"Oh, Karen," he said. "I hope we didn't wake you."

"Oh, no," I assured him. "I was relaxing and reading."

"I'm glad you came down. Fellow travelers need to meet under better circumstances," Caldwell said. "So sorry about last night for all of you. Not a good way to start a trip, is it?"

He reached out to pull me closer to the group. "Here are some fellow Americans—Betty and Barb, retired schoolteachers. We were just commiserating about Mr. Howard. They were quite good friends of his."

I turned and got my first good look at the Betty and Barb, and quite a pair they were: matching large women in their late sixties with tightly curled steel-gray hair, blue polyester blazers, tie-on shoes, large wire-rimmed glasses, and, just to be different, one was wearing a red scarf at her neck and the other a yellow one. They were both still crying, but the sound had subsided to a soft burble.

"Hello," I said. I hadn't caught which one was Betty and which was Barb, and I wondered if it really mattered. The Tweedles.

"We were so looking forward to spending time with Howard again. Every year we meet here for the Chelsea Flower Show."

"It's been ten years now. A kind of anniversary for us. We had so many things planned."

"You know his wife doesn't like flowers, so we would have had him all to ourselves."

"Just like old times."

"At least we did see him for a moment."

"When we came in late last night."

"We popped our heads in and said hello. He was so pleased to see us."

"But he was reading and we didn't want to bother him, so we left him there all alone."

"Maybe we shouldn't have."

They both started to weep, as if on cue.

I was trying to keep them separate, but they were blurring together. I was even having trouble telling which of them was speaking; their lips barely moved, and I always seemed to be looking at the wrong one when a remark was uttered.

"Girls," Caldwell called them and pointed at me. "Please meet Karen Nash. She's a mystery writer."

I sat down with a hard thump in the other high-backed chair in the room. I thought I had told him I was incognito. This lie was becoming a tourniquet around my neck. Even my metaphors were getting twisted.

"Well, then maybe she can find out what happened to Howard," said one of them. I guessed it was Barb.

"Oh, Barb, it was simply Howard's time. We must accept this," said the one who I was now sure was Betty.

Barb was wearing the red scarf and Betty the yellow.

"But there's nothing to find out," I started, then added, "He died of a heart attack. Isn't that right, Caldwell?"

Caldwell turned slowly to me, his face ashen. "He did, but we've just had news. Apparently the doctor took it upon himself to check his level of digoxin, which Mr. Worth was taking to regulate his heart, and found that it was quite high. High enough to bring on a heart attack."

"How awful," I said. "What can this mean? I've heard that that medication can be very tricky."

"It might be a simple matter of doubling up his dose," Caldwell suggested. "He might have forgotten and taken it again."

"Yes, of course," I said. "Tired from jet lag, getting off of his normal schedule. That makes total sense."

"Or that awful snit of a wife might have slipped it to him," Betty said in her flat Nebraskan voice. "And killed him."

FOURTEEN

The Richest Blend

When I woke the next day my first thought was, *Had Howard Worth been murdered?* I tried to remind myself that it had nothing to do with me, although I was the one who found him, and, somehow, that tied me to his death in an oddly emotional way.

In those few moments when I'd struggled with the fact that he was dead, I had wanted to save him. I remembered my Girl Scout training, my Lifesavers' Code, my CPR lessons—but all for naught. He could not have been reached or revived by the time I found him.

But maybe I could do something to find out what had actually happened to him—how he had died. Learning his death was accidental would clear my mind and relieve me; if, however, I discovered that it was a result of foul play, I would be able to see that justice was served.

Also, because of my horrid thoughts about doing away with Dave, I had begun to suspect ordinary people capable of awful things. What if someone close to Howard had done him in? Unfortunately this now seemed plausible to me.

I decided a few questions to Annette and the Tweedles wouldn't hurt anything. Gentle, but probing. I knew how to do that, like trying to help someone find the perfect book at the library, ask around the edges.

I stretched in bed. I was also worried about what Guy meant by his gesture to me outside the museum—was there any chance he had taken me seriously and was trying to involve himself with Dave? Anxiety often attacked me in the early morning when I was drowsy and vulnerable. I tried to push this thought away.

Yes, I hated that lousy plumber. Yes, he had done me wrong. Even yes, I had said I wanted him dead. But I no longer wanted to be involved with him in any way, and killing him would certainly be just one more way of staying tied to him. One, in fact, that could send me to prison. I imagined myself for a moment as a prison librarian, wondering what selection of books they would have, seeing myself raising the quality of the books for the inmates. But I quickly decided all connections must be broken.

I loved staying in bed for a while after I woke up. It felt like such a luxury. That was one more thing I hadn't liked about Dave. He would go from snoring to sitting bolt upright in seconds. I swear, a minute later he was drinking coffee and reading the paper or talking on the phone. Plumbers get up early, he had explained to me. Toilets wait for no one.

Often, in the morning, I figured things out—a better way to check in books, how to organize the new display in the children's reading room.

This morning I started a list of questions to ask the members of this temporary household about Howard Worth's last night while waiting for the other inhabitants to come to life.

Finally I heard someone stirring in the house; a door closed, and gentle steps sounded on the stairs. I was sure it was Caldwell. I had a feeling the Tweedles would be sleeping in late. This was my chance to have a little alone time with him. I doubted it was

Annette, because I knew the doctor had given her a bottle of sedatives. She would not be up too early.

As I slid out of bed and my feet hit the floor, I felt much more in the world than I had yesterday. Ten hours of sleep minus three pints of beer will do that for one. The weather looked fine outside; clouds scudded across the sky, but they were fluffy and not at all threatening.

I pulled on a pair of jeans and a gray sweater that was a nice neutral. I washed my face, brushed my teeth, put a dab of lipstick on for color and declared myself ready to meet the day.

When I opened my door, I found a tray with a pot of tea, a white mug, and a pitcher of milk on it.

Something in me melted. I knew that Caldwell was only doing for me what he did for all his guests, but it felt good to be taken care of.

I picked up the tray and carefully went down the stairs with it. Caldwell was humming a piece of Mozart in the kitchen as he plunked some bread down in the toaster. The soft sound of his voice lifted me up.

He hadn't seen me yet, so I stood and watched him, how gracefully he moved around the kitchen, putting the toast in a basket and getting plates out of the cupboards. His light brown curly hair formed a cowl around his head. He was wearing a plain white baker's apron and had a tea towel tucked through the tie. But what I was really noticing was how content he was.

"Very professional," I said.

He jumped at the sound of my voice, then turned and smiled. "Good morning. What am I professional about?"

I nodded at his outfit.

"This is the way that Jacques says to have one's towel always at the ready." He pulled out the towel he had tucked into his apron strings.

"Pepin?" I asked.

"Who else, but the master chef himself."

"Do you mind if I have my tea down here? With you?"

"Please do. Why don't you go settle in the sitting room and I'll bring you something in a moment." He looked up from what he was doing and gave me a once-over. "My, you look lovely today."

Again, something inside of me let go—a huge chunk of ice that I had been keeping in the deep freeze sloughed off. I said, as my mother had taught me, "Thank you."

The windows of the back room faced west, so the sun wasn't streaming in, but rather the new morning light was tipping the tops of the trees in the garden and they looked as if they'd been gilded. I poured myself a cup of Caldwell's strong tea, topped it off with a healthy dose of full-fat milk, and drank.

Caldwell brought in a basket of toast, a slab of butter, and marmalade. "In case you want a little edge to your sweet," he said.

Even the smell of the toast satisfied me. "Thank you. This is very nice to be waited on."

"It's a pleasure. How are you this fine day?" he asked after he poured himself a cup of tea and sank back contentedly into his high-backed chair. He was holding the cup of tea in both hands close to his face, looking almost as if he was ready to dive into it.

"Isn't that the chair that Howard died in?" I pointed out.

Caldwell dipped his head. "Yes, but it's not the chair's fault. Not that I'm not sorry about the tragedy of Mr. Worth's death. It must have been terrible for you to find him here."

"Yes and no. For a moment, I wanted to revive him so badly, but then there was also something peaceful about his death. He was simply gone from the husk that was his body. I had never felt that so clearly before."

"That's beautifully said. Again, I hear the writer in you."

"I guess the only thing that bothers me now is

how did he happen to ingest too much digitalis. You knew him fairly well?"

"Yes," Caldwell nodded thoughtfully. "As much as anyone could know that man. He's been staying with me for the last ten years when he comes to the show."

"Would you say he was a careless man?"

"Not at all. I would have described him as meticulous." He stopped as he seemed to see where I was going. "But we all make mistakes, don't remember how many sugars we've put in our tea, that sort of thing."

"Yes, I suppose we do. But having too sweet tea is a rather different thing than overdosing on a drug." I could tell I was making him very uncomfortable.

He stood up abruptly. "And what's on your agenda today?"

Suddenly, my mind went over my itinerary. I remembered what I had planned for Dave and me on our third night in London. A play. For wasn't this city the leading theater capital of the English-speaking world? Where better to see Shakespeare performed? I had two tickets to *Macbeth* at the Globe this evening. Two tickets.

"*Macbeth*," I blurted.

"Indeed. Not at the Globe!" he said with delight in his voice.

"Yes. But unfortunately I have an extra ticket, you know, for my traveling companion who isn't here."

"Oh," he said.

His utterance hung in the air. It sounded hopeful. I wondered if he might like to join me.

"Would you—" I started.

"I don't suppose—" he began at the same moment.

"Maybe you might—" I continued.

"I've nothing on," he said.

"Please join me," I said.

"I'd love to," he acquiesced.

As soon as that was settled, I felt I needed to ask him about Guy, how I could get in touch with him. I was regretting my conversation with him, the sense that he might do something bad to Dave.

"I wanted to ask you—" I was interrupted by a stampede happening above our heads.

"Oh, the Tweedles are coming," he murmured. "I must warn you. They're quite rambunctious in the morning."

"When aren't they?"

"Don't worry. They go to bed fairly early, and they often have a doze in the afternoon."

Down the stairs the women came, sounding like many more than two, and into the sitting room. Again, they were dressed similarly, but not identically. Solid brown walking shoes, navy blue polyester pants, white shirts under gray cardigans. Your basic Catholic schoolgirl outfit. But they had different colored scarves around their necks—one red and one purple. If I could put a name to a scarf, I would be able to tell them apart.

"Here we are," one of them announced as they clattered into the room.

"We are here," the other said and then they both began to titter, an odd sound coming from two such large women.

"Good morning, my dears," Caldwell said. "How does a cuppa sound?"

"Don't you love the way he talks?" Red Scarf said to me as she sat down on the love seat.

"Swell," said Purple Scarf.

"Toast, just the way we like it," said Red Scarf as she accepted a plate from Caldwell.

After they were settled with their cups of tea, Purple said to me, brushing crumbs off her chin, "I suppose what's happened to dear Howard is giving you ideas for your next book."

I slid into mystery writer mode. "I'm doing some research here in London for a new book. Yes. And I can't help being curious about Mr. Worth's demise."

"You must be very smart. I can't believe we're really meeting a real writer." She nudged the other

Tweedle. "Who knows what she's thinking about?"

I wasn't quite sure what to say to that. I simply nodded and swallowed the remains of my tea, which had gone rather cold. "You two have known Mr. Worth for so long."

They looked at each other, then started blinking tears away.

One said, "I still can't believe it."

"It's a bad dream."

"He was such a worthy man."

"So knowledgeable about flowers."

"Not another like him."

"Annette had no idea what he was made of."

"Why, she wouldn't know a petunia from a begonia."

Somehow I felt compelled to defend the new wife. "But she knew how to take care of him."

"Did she?" Red Scarf asked.

"She didn't manage that very well. He's dead," added Purple Scarf. "As they say, there's proof in the pudding."

I decided to come right out and ask them what they were insinuating. "What would she have to gain from killing him?"

In unison they said, "His money."

Then Purple Scarf filled me in. "You might not know this about Howard, but he had hybridized a dark purple, almost blue rose. Worth millions, that flower is. No one had thought it could even be done."

"I'm sure given another few years he might have succeeded at the impossible."

"A blue rose."

They both fell silent at the thought of such an accomplishment.

After a moment, Red Scarf came out of the trance. "Don't let us keep you. You must be a very busy woman, with your murders and all.

"Maybe she'll put us in her next book." She nudged Purple. "Wouldn't that be a hoot!"

They both tittered as I backed out of the room. At least they had stopped crying. Caldwell followed me into the hallway.

"Were you about to ask me something earlier? Before the descent of the Tweedles?"

"Yes. Could you tell me how to get in touch with that man I met the other night? You know, the blond-haired man at the pub? He said his name was Guy," I said, hoping to have another chance to talk to him.

"You mean the bloke you had the discussion with?"

"Yes," I said.

Caldwell confirmed my fear. "I don't really know

him. Don't even know his last name. I've had him pointed out to me a few times."

"Is he a regular at that pub, do you think?"

"Yes, I've seen him there quite a few times before. I think someone told me that he was in the crime business. Was he helping you with your research? Did you need to ask him a few more questions?"

"Just one," I answered as I wondered what my chances were of finding Guy again.

FIFTEEN

The Flower World

As I came out of my room, all ready for the day, with my good walking shoes on, Annette Worth opened the door to her room at the same time. She looked much better than the last time I had seen her—her dark hair was pulled up high in a pony-tail, and she had on a red sweater and a navy skirt; she was even wearing a light shade of lipstick. She had probably packed no clothes appropriate for mourning.

"Hi," I said, not knowing if she would want to talk, but dying to ask her some questions.

She stepped toward me, almost hesitantly, and took my arm. "You were so helpful at the time of Howard's death. I still think of you finding him. I'm so glad it was you and not me."

I wasn't sure how to answer that statement so I said, "You're looking much better today."

She blushed slightly and slid her hands down her sweater. "Thank you. It's all show. Inside I'm torn up. But I have to go to this Chelsea Flower Show and make the rounds for Howard. A friend of Howard's is going to help me with everything. Tony. I don't know what I'd do without him. I have to accept some kind of award on Howard's behalf. He would have wanted that."

"I'm sure." I decided I might as well ask her a couple questions since she seemed open to chatting. "I heard that the doctor called with a toxicology report. They think he took too much digitalis?"

She shook her head and then said, "I know they think that, but it doesn't seem possible."

"How so?"

"Well, I'm a nurse and I give Howard all his medications. I know exactly what he was taking and when he was taking it. I gave him his usual dose right at nine o'clock, like I always do."

"He couldn't have taken an extra one himself?"

"I'm in charge of his medications. They're in my

bags. The only way he could have taken an extra dose of digitalis was to sneak into the room after I had fallen asleep and take another pill. But why would he have done that?"

"Might he have wanted something else, like a sleeping pill, and taken the digitalis by accident?"

A horrified look pulled at her face. "I never thought of that. He was complaining that he couldn't go to sleep. That's why he stayed up so late reading."

Why, indeed, I wondered. "Is there any other explanation?"

"I've been afraid to think about it," she confessed. "It's occurred to me that someone might have poisoned him."

"But who and why? Not to mention how?"

She looked up at me and her eyes grew round. "Oh, many people were jealous of Howard. He had enemies in the flower world because of his new rose. He named it after me: Almost Blue Annette. It was the closest anyone had ever come to creating a blue rose. That was his hope, his desire, to hybridize a blue rose."

"And you think someone might have killed him over a flower? Sounds a bit extreme."

"You don't know this flower world. They are ruthless when it comes to their plants."

"But how would they have given him the digitalis? There was no one here that night but you, me, Caldwell, and the Tweedles."

"The Tweedles?" she asked.

"I'm sorry. I meant Barb and Betty."

"Yes," she said, tapping her lips. "Betty and Barb."

"But surely they're harmless?"

"Oh, I'm not suggesting anything. But one of them—I can never keep them apart—was in love with Howard before I came along."

SIXTEEN

❧

Bangers and Mash

At 11:00 A.M., I was standing at the door of the Cock and Bull when the pub owner unlocked it and walked outside with a sign that said open. The place was empty, as I had hoped.

After my filling breakfast at Caldwell's, I had gone for a long walk along the Thames, the kind of walk I had dreamed of for years, moseying in and out of narrow winding streets, staring at house after house of brick and stone with flowerpots on balconies, and wooden benches facing the river. The day was clear and warm. I went farther than I had intended, but didn't get lost because the river was always there, guiding me.

By the time I got back to Caldwell's neighborhood and found the pub, I had been walking for a couple of hours. My feet were blistered, my legs were aching, and I was absolutely famished.

"Love, have a seat. You look knackered," the bartender said, wiping the counter in front of me.

I pulled up a stool and sat at the bar. I thought of the word *knackered*—a term usually employed for putting a horse down for dog food. Maybe one could also use it for taking an old man out as he sat reading. Not a very nice word.

"What can I get for you?"

"I'd love a half-pint of beer, but I really need something to eat."

"The menu's up there." He pointed to a small sign at the rear of the bar scrawled in a hard-to-read hand.

I squinted my eyes and tried to make it out, but the words were nearly unintelligible and even when I deciphered them, I wasn't sure what they meant. Finally I asked, "What's good?"

"Bangers and mash."

I nodded. While I had often heard of this dish, I had never tasted it. The name alone made me curious, and, as I had come this far, I might as well try it.

"What would you like to drink?"

Another decision. I remembered Caldwell explaining to me that each pub was licensed by a particular brewery. "Whatever you recommend."

After some consideration, the bartender came to a decision and drew me a half-pint. I had learned my lesson and this one small beer was going to be my limit. If I had more I would nap all afternoon. But I was on vacation.

When I took my first sip, I was surprised how good the dark brew tasted. The other night I hadn't really noticed much about the beer—but then it had been after eating spicy Indian food and being overwhelmed by everything around me. This beer tasted fuller in flavor than any I had tasted in America.

As I was getting ready to ask the bartender about Guy, he disappeared. When he came back through what I assumed was the kitchen door, he was carrying a plate filled with white and brown food. As he approached, I could see that it was a pile of mashed potatoes, the "mash," and two thick round sausages, the "bangers." Quite stolid food for the middle of the day, but I was famished. I had decided that I would in no way be on a diet for this trip.

"Mustard?" the bartender asked.

"Please."

I tasted the mash. Quite good. Very mashy, with

a hint of cream. Then a bite of the banger. The sausage was oily and bland, but not bad. The tang of the mustard would serve it well.

The bartender set the mustard down. "All right, luv?"

I waved my fork at him, wanting him to stay long enough for me to swallow a bite of banger. "I was wondering," I started, but wasn't quite sure how to describe Guy.

"There was a gentleman in here two nights ago," I went on.

"Yes, I think I was working that night."

"He sat over there," I pointed to the corner.

"Go on."

"About your height, blond hair, maybe mid-thirties. Wore a suit coat. Looked rather professional. His first name is Guy."

"What did he drink?"

I wondered if he was serious. "I think he was having a glass of red wine."

"Oh, him. Sits over in the corner. Yeah, he comes by now and again. Not exactly what you would call a regular. Don't know much more than that about him, but I know who you mean."

"You don't by any chance know his full name?"

"Not really."

"Do you know what he does?"

The bartender leaned over the counter and lowered his voice. "Odd you should ask. I've wondered that myself. He looks quite clean and on the up-and-up but you should see some of the people he meets here. Not our usual clientele, I'll tell you that. I've heard rumor that he's involved in some fairly shady business. Why? Did he do something to you?"

"Oh, no. Nothing like that. No. We had an exchange and I asked him about something and I was wondering if he had checked it out. I wanted to get in touch with him. When does he tend to come here?"

"It's hard to say. It's a bit one-and-off. He'll be here right steady for a while and then might not see him for a fortnight."

"Oh," I said, very disappointed.

"He wasn't here last night. Like I said, it's hard to know when he'll show up again."

"Yes, I see." I wouldn't be able to visit to the pub that night, as I was going to *Macbeth* with Caldwell. Although maybe afterward.

The bartender leaned forward, trying to help me out. "Would you like to leave a message for him?"

"That would be great." I reached into my purse for a pen and tore a piece of paper from the notebook I always carried with me.

"Don't let your food get cold now."

"No, I won't." I cut off a hunk of banger and dipped it in the mustard while I thought of what to write. Nothing incriminating, but something that would give him the right message.

"From the woman whose ex-boyfriend was a plumber," I wrote and then reread the sentence. How pathetic that definition seemed. How had that happened to me? I continued, "Please forget about what we talked about. I'm feeling much better about everything. Thanks for listening." I signed my name and wrote down my cell phone number, in case he had any questions.

Feeling relieved, I walked back toward Caldwell's house full of meat and potatoes and beer. A nice combination. In no hurry, I ambled, looking in all the shopwindows, browsing as I went. Somehow even pots and pans looked more interesting in England. Every single object seemed to have more style.

A few blocks away from the B and B, I came across a clothing store and walked into the Chic Boutique. At home, shopping for clothes wasn't my favorite pastime, but having a new dress or, as they called it, a new "frock" from London might be very smart.

The shop was barely big enough to turn around in, but brimming with clothes: racks of dresses and tops. Shelves to the ceiling packed with scarves and sweaters. I looked at a few garments, but all the clothes looked way too young for me. Too small, too bright, too fussy.

As I was ready to walk out, a young woman with bright red hair, brighter red lips, and an immense smile popped up from behind the counter. "Hello, hello," she sang out.

"Hi," I said, startled into being a stodgy American.

"Looking for something special?" she asked and came around the counter. She was wearing tight, slashed jeans, and an orange top that clashed with all her redness but somehow still managed to look very good on her.

"Oh, not really. Just looking," I mumbled, quite overcome by her vibrancy.

Orangina, as I named her in my mind, walked around in front of me, getting between me and the door. "Hmmm, we have some new colors in that would suit you perfectly."

I looked down at the clothes I was wearing: brown walking shoes, jeans, gray sweater. Orangina didn't seem at all impressed that the warm gray color of the sweater I was wearing complemented my eyes.

"You'd look lovely in a dark red. Are you going anyplace special?"

"I'm going to the theater tonight."

"Perfect. Wait till you see what I have for you. Came in not a moment ago." She ran through a door behind the register, rummaged around, and came back out carrying a package.

In a dramatic gesture, she unwrapped the package and swirled out the garment. A lacy-knit shawl.

I fell in love the moment I saw it. It was a deep burgundy, the color of overripe cherries, and so soft looking you just wanted to touch it, stroke it. I reached out for it, then pulled my hand back.

"But I don't wear shawls," I blurted out.

"Why ever not? They're perfect for you. Elegant, but casual. Simple. That's your style. But you could get more richness in your wardrobe. Some people think that you must give up style for comfort. You can have both." As she was saying all this she had walked forward and was wrapping me in the shawl, swaddling me in it.

She turned me to face the full-length mirror.

I have always loved makeovers. One of my guilty pleasures. A plain or even unattractive woman who gets a new haircut, puts on some makeup, takes off her glasses, smiles, and becomes a beauty. I find them hopeful and fascinating. But I had never known it could be done so quickly and so easily.

When I looked into the mirror, I saw a new person. The shawl had transformed me. My hair had turned darker, my eyes deeper, my skin rosier. I felt as if I had even grown an inch or two. I looked like I knew something secret and divine.

I had changed into Glam Librarian.

There was no question about buying the shawl. I didn't even look at the price tag, something I had never not done before in my life. I didn't care what it cost. I just handed her my card. That luscious burgundy wrap was going home with me.

In fact, it was hard for me to take the shawl off. But finally I handed it over to Orangina and she wrapped it in tissue paper and put in a box.

"Ciao," she said to me as I left the shop with the shawl tucked safely under my arm.

I couldn't help peeking at the receipt as I walked away. What I saw made me swallow hard—nearly a week's salary. I couldn't believe what I had done.

I hoped Caldwell would like it.

SEVENTEEN

Favorite Tragedy

I stood in front of the bathroom mirror, the only mirror in my suite. I was wearing my simple black dress made of some chemical compound that was guaranteed never to wrinkle. After bandaging a blister, I had put on shoes with a small heel that were very comfortable to walk in. In honor of the occasion, I had lined my eyes with a soft black pencil and dabbed on concealer to hide the worst of my shadows. My hair I had washed and set loosely on rollers and now it was curling around my ears. All this was very nice and I looked completely presentable.

Then I brought out the shawl. With my eyes closed, I wrapped it around my shoulders, felt its warmth embrace me.

When I opened my eyes, the transformation was complete. Another woman stood before me. Someone who didn't wear a watch. Someone who knew how to have a good time. Someone who might even drink champagne if it were offered.

I dabbed my lips with a color that came close to the warm red of the shawl. Even better.

I was ready to go.

As I descended the stairs, I felt like I was going to prom, an event I had never taken part in. My junior year I had not been invited; my senior year a fellow intellectual who worked on the school paper asked me out to see *Woodstock*. It was my second time seeing the movie and his third. No way would we condescend to go to such a bourgeois event as prom. But I have forever missed being given the opportunity to wear a frothy confection of a dress.

Unbeknownst to me, the Tweedles awaited. They came out from the sitting room and looked me up and down. Caldwell was not yet in sight.

"My oh my. Are you going to be warm enough?" one of them asked.

"And those shoes look a little high. You be careful or you'll twist your ankle in those. Betty and I insist

on wearing our walking shoes no matter what the affair. Don't we, Betty?"

"Absolutely. I'd hate to have to deal with the British health system. You'd probably have to wait days
to be seen. And miss all that time on your vacation."

I looked down at myself. The shawl was awfully
lightweight and the shoes were a little higher than I
was accustomed to. Had I made a mistake?

Right then Caldwell walked out from the
kitchen. He was saying to the Tweedles, "You can't
miss it. It's right at the end of the road and it has a
huge banner. I'm sure you'll enjoy your meal."

He stopped when he saw me. At first he didn't
say anything, but the warmth in his eyes was
enough.

Finally he said, "You are a vision. Perfectly perfect."

No one had ever used the word *perfect* to describe me before, even though it was something I
constantly strived to be.

Caldwell was wearing a dark navy blazer over a
dark sweater with a paisley silk scarf. To my eye, he
looked very European. Debonair in a way that American men rarely dared to be.

We took Caldwell's Smart car, which I had never
seen before. It looked like it would fold up and fit

into a purse. I loved it. Because it took up just half a parking space, he managed to tuck it into a spot that was only a few blocks away from the Globe.

When we stepped out on the sidewalk, he took my arm and tucked it under his. While the air was chilly, I was completely warm.

"How do you feel about *Macbeth*?" he asked as we walked.

"While I think it's an important play," I said. "It's not my favorite of the tragedies."

"What is?"

"Depends on the day."

He laughed. "I know what you mean. On this day, which is your favorite?"

"I'm not sure, but it's always between *Othello* and *Lear*. *Othello* is more romantic but *Lear* seems to me to be a truer tragedy. An unavoidable one."

"How so?"

"We all grow old. We all fear we are not loved."

He patted my hand. "How did you get to be this wise?"

"I just sound like I know what I'm talking about. It comes with the territory," I said, thinking of my job, answering questions about books all day long.

"What territory?" he asked.

I realized I had slipped, but it could be fixed. "You know, sounding smart and authorial."

"Of course."

We rounded a corner and stopped.

There stood the Globe, an almost exact duplicate of the theater in which Shakespeare's plays had first been presented, dark beams crisscrossing the white stucco façade. Three stories high, the building was an open-air amphitheater about a hundred feet in diameter.

Staring up at it, I felt transported back five hundred years. I wondered if the people then felt as excited as I did on entering this enormous theater.

I had read up on it, of course. The original Globe Theatre was able to hold about three thousand people, if one counted the people standing in the "pit," the open area right in front of the stage.

"I can't believe I'm actually seeing this place for real. Something I've read about forever. It's as if the books, the plays, even Shakespeare himself, have come to life right before my eyes."

"I know how you feel," Caldwell said, giving my arm a squeeze as we walked forward.

I believed he did. I put my hand on top of his and squeezed back.

I was entering a fairy-tale world.

Enchanted.

EIGHTEEN

That Damn Spot!

Walking into the Globe Theatre to see *Macbeth* on the arm of a handsome Brit, I determined nothing was going to keep me from enjoying this once-in-a-lifetime evening.

The center of the new Globe was like that of the old—roofless, open to the stars. With a thrust stage and a large, open yard, the area had seating only around the periphery. I had purchased the best seats money—thirty-three pounds, to be exact—could buy: middle-gallery, front-row seats, a splurge, but one I was very happy I had made when Caldwell

murmured his delight at where we were sitting. The
seats were plain wooden benches, but Caldwell insisted on hiring cushions for us to sit on.

He handed me into the row and followed behind as we made our way to the exact center. I had
planned it this way. I wanted to be able to see everything. With the pillars in the roofed area, many
of the views were compromised. But I also knew
that I needed to be sitting. There was no way I
could have stood in the middle yard for the three
hours of a play. They allowed absolutely no form
of stool or folding chair and, out in the open, if it
rained, they didn't allow umbrellas. But the play
would go on.

"I'm very sorry for your companion that he will be
missing this, but I can't help but be happy for myself," Caldwell said as we sat shoulder to shoulder.

"I think you will probably enjoy it more than
he would have," I said quietly, knowing Dave. He
would have found the seats too small, the play too
long, and would have fidgeted through the first half
of the play and slept through the second half.

"Do you come here often?" I asked.

He paused and said curtly, "Not recently."

I wondered what I had stirred up, but didn't feel
like intruding. I looked around and marveled at the
theater, the people filing in and beginning to fill up

the middle area. The theater being open to the sky reminded me of an outdoor baseball game. I decided not to pass this thought along to Caldwell as it made me sound too American. I was gawking, but I didn't care. Sometimes one had to give in and simply be a tourist.

"What do you think?" Caldwell asked me.

"I'm sure it wasn't quite like this in Shakespeare's day, but it certainly gives the feeling."

"Yes, I'm afraid the original might have been a little more rowdy. At that time, this theater was in the red-light district. Plays were considered quite risqué."

"Well, acting was, after all, a purple profession. Shakespeare was lucky that he was being patronized by the Lord Chamberlain."

"My, my. Aren't you a little font of knowledge?" Caldwell teased me.

Again, I almost blurted out that it was because I was a librarian, but caught myself in time. This pretending to be something I was not was wearing very thin. "I was an English major. I guess some of the facts just stuck."

Before I could say anything more, the sound of a lute filled the air. With little ceremony and no damping of the floodlights that shone on the grounds of the theater, the three witches backed onto the stage, circling around, staring out at the crowd, and then turning to each other.

The first witch, with long dark hair tied back with a rope of thorns, asked, "When shall we three meet again / In thunder, lightning, or in rain?"

The next witch cackled out, "When the hurly-burly's done, / When the battle's lost and won."

I sank into the words. They hit me hard and I felt myself swimming in their power, especially the second witch's lines. *Hurly-burly* was so full of sounds, and I loved the sense of the battle lost, then won. Life in a nutshell.

I slipped a glance at Caldwell. He was leaning forward but must have sensed my look, for he turned and crinkled his eyes, then quickly went back to watching the play. I, too, lost myself in it.

That was, until Lady Macbeth entered the scene. She was tall and regal, wearing a murderously dark crimson gown that spoke of rich beauty and danger. Sweeping into the room, she read the letter from Macbeth and came to a decision as to what must happen. When Macbeth entered her room, she stood taller than he was and with more majesty.

Then she uttered the lines: "Look like the innocent flower, / But be the serpent under't," and I was struck by what was happening in this play. She was conspiring to kill a man.

I had just found a dead man, a man someone might well have killed. And hadn't I, in my mind at least, thought to do the same? And, while under the influence of too much to drink, talked about it to someone who might be able to arrange such a thing? What had I been thinking?

I was chilled to my bones and shivered slightly.

Caldwell turned and asked if I wanted his jacket. I wrapped my shawl around my shoulders and assured him I was fine. Of all the plays to see, why was I watching this one? If only I had managed to find the blond man and explain myself to him and tell him not to worry about the plumber anymore. Or if only I knew for sure that he would receive my note.

I tried to shake off my worries, thinking how ridiculous I was being. After all, the man probably knew I had been a bit tipsy, and why would he do anything to Dave, a man he didn't even know or care about?

And having found Howard Worth dead, even suspecting that he might have been killed by someone who was sleeping in the same house as I was. It was all too much.

When Lady Macbeth, wringing her hands, said, "Yet who would have thought the old man to have had so much blood in him," I was struck again with worry and wonder at how I was hearing this play as if for the first time.

In that moment, I knew that Lady Macbeth was amazed at the humanness of a dying man. I was seeing this play with wide-open eyes. How could I have even thought of killing another human being, even for a moment? Horror washed over me.

I stood up without realizing I had moved.

Caldwell asked, "Are you okay?"

"I need some air." But even as I said the words, I saw that I couldn't get out of the row in the middle of a scene. I sank down in my seat.

Caldwell put his hand on the small of my back and advised me to lean forward and breathe deeply. I fell forward in my chair, almost touching my knees with my head. Saying a mantra, "Nothing has happened," to myself, I calmed down. I had gotten too caught up in the play. My life was not like that. I was not a queen. Not a murderer, but had I set in motion something that was unstoppable? No, it was only a "dagger of the mind."

After a few moments, I was able to sit back up.

Caldwell gave me a worried look. "All right?"

"I'm fine," I whispered back.

For the rest of the play, I kept myself at a bit of a remove, watching the people watching the play, noticing the fine night it was, the music, the warmth of Caldwell sitting next to me. A historic magical play about a time that never was, I reminded myself. Such dark deeds would never happen because of me.

"You gave me a bit of a scare in there," Caldwell said as we walked back to his car.

"I'm sorry. I don't know what came over me. I never get faint like that, but all of a sudden it all seemed to hit me."

"Probably jet lag and overstimulation. Being in a new country as well."

"That's it. I lead a quiet life at home."

"I suppose you'd like to go back to your room," he said with slight reluctance in his voice.

"Well, actually, I was hoping we could swing by the Cock and Bull. As I recall, I owe you a pint."

"Are you sure?" He brightened up.

"It would be my pleasure. After all, you drove."

"Yes, but you provided the tickets."

"You were gracious enough to accompany me."

He stopped in the street for a moment and looked at me. "If I didn't know better, I'd swear that you were British. You can acquiesce with the best of them."

There in the middle of the street, I dropped him a curtsy. "I thank you, my lord, for those kind words."

He took my hand and raised me up. "And now, on to the libations."

NINETEEN

Companion?

We found a table easily at the Cock and Bull. Caldwell offered to go up and get the drinks.

"Only one tonight for me. I learned my lesson. But a full pint if you don't mind." I handed him a ten-pound note.

Caldwell refused to take it and tried to walk away.

I grabbed the back of his sports coat and stopped him.

"Caldwell, I insist. If you do not let me pay my round, I can never go out for a beer with you again."

A laugh shouted out of him. I never would have imagined he had such a hearty guffaw. When he calmed down, he wiped his eyes and said, "I swear, you are as conniving as any Englishwoman I have ever known."

"Again with the compliments." I held out the note and this time he took it. The pub was quieter than the last night we had been there. In an easy glance, I perused the room and did not find my man lurking in any corner. Disappointment prickled me. I wanted to talk to Guy and be done with this whole matter. The way he had said he'd take care of Dave couldn't help but worry me. I never wanted to think about Dave the plumber again.

Caldwell came back carefully carrying two brimming pints of bitter. With a night off and having my English legs under me, I was looking forward to savoring the drink.

He sat down opposite me, handed me my pint, lifted his toward me. I followed suit. We clinked glasses and he said, "Here's to you and the man who brought you."

"That would be yourself."

"I hope so." He smiled and we drank.

"Caldwell, have you ever been to America?" I asked him, realizing how little I knew about him.

"Oh, I suppose I have," he said with a shrug.

I wondered if he had actually heard my question. "How's that?"

"Well, I've only ever visited New York and from what I've heard that's not really America."

I nodded. "It certainly bears little resemblance to the Midwest, where I'm from."

"Have you always lived there? In the Middle West?"

"Yup, the heart of the country. Born in St. Paul, Minnesota. Have you always lived in London?"

He shook his head. "No, I'm from Basingstoke."

"Where's that?"

"Not far, southwest of London. Not exactly in the country, but certainly not urban."

"How long have you lived in London?"

"Most of my adult life. I came here for my first job."

"What was that?"

"Oh, nothing really. A way to get my foot in the door."

"How long have you had the B and B?"

"It's over ten years, I believe."

"What made you go into this business?"

"Well, I was semiretired, and my partner, Sally, inherited this house. It's expensive to own a house in London. After thinking it over, we decided to make it pay for itself."

I took a long draw on the beer. Sally. "What happened to her?"

"Oh, it's a sad story."

"Like *Macbeth*?"

He looked away. "Not quite as tortured as that. A handsome older man came to stay after the B and B had been open a couple of years. He was rich and promised her many things, but he was a bit of a ninny if you ask me. Sal was quite taken with him. At first I found it amusing."

I sat still, waiting for him to go on.

"Not at all amusing when I came home to find our savings cleaned out, the house supposedly signed over to me, which was generous, and Sal gone off with Howard."

A moment later, the name registered. "Wait a minute. Did you say Howard?"

He nodded.

"Howard Worth?"

"The same."

"But he's married to Annette."

"Yes, Sally's relationship with Howard didn't last long, but by the time they broke up she had fallen in love with America. She could be rather flighty. Plus, I didn't really want her back."

"Were you and Sally married?" I asked.

"We never bothered."

"Have you heard from her since?"

"Just a postcard. She's living in Chicago."

"Oh, I'm really sorry," I said, but I wasn't. Nice to hear the story of his last love and see that he was over it. One did get over breakups—I hoped. But it concerned me that Howard had been involved.

"It's for the best. She wasn't much good at being a host. She liked fitting out the rooms, but hated it when the guests made a mess in them."

I took a large swallow of my beer, then asked the question I needed the answer to. "How did that make you feel about Howard?"

"Oh, I didn't really blame him. I think she was ready to bolt. If it hadn't been him, it would have been someone else."

"Awfully civilized of you," I said, although I was rather skeptical of how evenly he talked about the breakup.

"I try." He raised his eyebrows at me.

"Rather ironic that he would end up dying in your B and B," I murmured.

"Yes, I hope the police don't find it so. But it sounds like he died of natural causes." He was silent for a moment, then turned his eyes on me and asked, "Now that you know about my last affair, tell me about your no-show companion."

I almost spit my beer out. Did he know that Dave

had split up with me? For some reason I was still not ready to talk about it. He handed me a linen handkerchief that he pulled out from his pocket. "Breathe, Karen."

I gasped and sputtered and when I was done, he was still waiting. "My companion?" I asked, weakly.

"Yes, whoever was supposed to come with you. Who was he and why isn't he here?"

"Well, his name was Dave."

Caldwell jerked his head back, frowned and said, "Oh, I'm sorry. Do you mean he died?"

"Not really. I mean, no. I guess I spoke of him in the past tense because—" And here I stopped myself. Other than Rosie and Guy, I had told no one what had happened to me. I could not bring myself to talk about it. "I guess because he's not here with me at this moment, so he seems in the past."

Caldwell didn't say anything for a moment. Then he asked pleasantly, "And what does this man in your life do?"

"Dave's a plumber. We've been going out for a few years."

"Sounds rather serious." Caldwell touched his lip, then asked, "However did you happen to go out with a plumber, Karen? Doesn't seem your style at all. I'd expect you to be with a lawyer or a professor. Someone in letters."

I thought back to the first time I had seen Dave, standing at my front door with his large box of tools. "How else? He came to fix my toilet."

"Oh, I see. He made himself indispensable."

"You could say that." For a brief moment I thought of telling him the whole story of what was going on with Dave, how he had dumped me, how he was now with Honey, how I followed him to their hotel, talking to a strange man about him, but I couldn't bring myself to tell him. It painted too mean a picture of me. I wanted to continue to be the lovely woman who wore the gorgeous shawl. I tried to think of something nice to say about Dave. "He has his good points."

"One thing I can say for sure is—he has good taste," Caldwell murmured.

Caldwell offered to drop me off at the door, but I told him not to be silly. I didn't mind the walk.

He found a parking spot two blocks away and we started strolling back to his house. It was then that I realized how awkward the end of this evening might be. I mean, if this was a date, which I didn't really think it was, but if it was, what would we do at the door, or when we got inside. At what point did we say good night?

How odd to go out with someone and go home with them—to separate rooms.

As we walked along, Caldwell pointed out the businesses on the street: the little greengrocer on the corner, the Persian rug shop, the best place to get coffee that wasn't a Starbucks.

"I love all these shops to walk to," I said. At that moment, I was loving everything. "Where I live you have to get in a car to get anyplace."

"Yes, this is quite different. I sometimes only use the car once or twice a week."

I could see his house down at the end of the block. We walked slower.

Caldwell told me stories of the people whose houses we were passing: a young couple with twins, an old woman with cats, a family from India with their grandmother. We stopped and looked at some of the front gardens; the roses bloomed an orangey pink under the streetlights.

When we arrived at his house, he opened the gate for me. We walked up the steps together and then both of us stopped at the top, right in front of the door.

"This has been quite nice," he said, looking down at his shoes.

I stared down at his shoes too. They were well-polished black shoes. Maybe they were oxfords. "Yes, it has."

He took a step toward me and said, "Karen?"

I looked up at him, hoping that he might see how much I liked him, how much I wanted him to touch me.

The door sprang open in front of us. Standing there was a striking woman I had never seen before.

She said, "My Caldwell. Finally you are home."

TWENTY

Madame Frou-Frou

She was not exactly beautiful. Too thin, too sharp to be a true beauty, but she was dramatic, with dark hair pulled back in a swirl and dark eyes that flashed in the dim light and a small but full mouth. I guessed she was in her early forties and I was sure, from her accent, that she was French.

We stepped into the house and she moved in on Caldwell, delicately kissing him on both cheeks, then murmured, "So good to see you, *mon cheri*."

"Francine, you came a day early," he said.

"It just happened. I should have called to tell you.

I thought I'd surprise." She touched his scarf. "My, you're all dressed up. Very handsome."

"Yes, Francine, this is Karen. She's a writer from America. We went to see *Macbeth* at the Globe. She had an extra ticket."

"Very good. A writer?" She looked me up and down and I couldn't tell from her sharp gaze how I measured up. "An American writer? You write the romances, I suppose?"

"No, just mysteries."

"Oh, very good. This I like." She wrapped her arms around Caldwell's arm and said, "So good to get him out. He is such a person of the home."

I nodded, not really knowing what kind of person he was at all.

"Francine, I have to tell you, something terrible has happened," Caldwell started.

She pulled away from him. "What? Sally isn't back, is she?"

"No, but Howard—"

"Oh, you told me. So he is married. This is good. So nice that you two can be friends again."

"No, he died."

Francine raised her eyebrows. "But he was old."

"Yes, but he died here in my house."

"Oh, my poor Caldwell. That man will forever be bringing trouble to you. It is better he is gone."

"Francine," Caldwell reprimanded her.

"I know what will cheer you up. I brought the Gigondas—your favorite kind," she purred at him. "Is right now breathing."

It took me a second to realize she was talking about a bottle of wine. All I knew was that I wanted to get out of that hallway and upstairs to my room. I did not want to have to witness Francine making a fuss over Caldwell at the end of our nondate.

"Thanks for coming along," I said as I slipped around them and headed for the stairs.

"Wouldn't you like a glass of wine?" he asked.

Francine turned and seconded, "Please join us."

Her use of the word *us* was what stopped me from even considering joining them. If they were an "us," I did not want to know it tonight. I wanted to keep my memory of this evening.

"Maybe some other time. I'm exhausted." I reached the stairs and went up into the darkness. I stumbled down the hall and found the door to my room and unlocked it. Inside I turned on the light and leaned against the door, closing my eyes and imagining the kiss that Caldwell might have given me.

After scrubbing my face and brushing my teeth, I crawled into bed, but instead of feeling tired, my body felt tightly wired. I wasn't used to this level of activity, plus I was wishing I had stayed for a glass of wine.

I could hear Caldwell and Francine murmuring below me, and, while I wondered what they were talking about, I resisted eavesdropping. But something in me drooped. I had had such a nice night. With Caldwell. He was truly a gentle man. Then I'd learned that Howard had stolen his partner away. Even so, I couldn't believe he would have had anything to do with Howard's death. But what if he had?

I had to believe Howard's death was most likely still the result of an accidental overdose, no matter what Annette thought. Maybe she handed him two pills by mistake. Maybe he had taken one on his own earlier and then swallowed the one she gave him.

But if Caldwell was interested in this French hussy, this Madame Frou-Frou, I stood no chance with him. Plus, it was all too much for me right now.

The last thing I needed to do was fall for a man who lived halfway across the planet from me, who thought I was a mystery writer, and didn't know I had thought of killing my last beau. That final fact might put anyone off the thought of dating me.

Since it was 11:00 P.M. in London, it would be 5:00 P.M. in Sunshine Valley. Perfect timing. Rosie always took a break at five. She was religiously structured about her day. Five o'clock was time for her cup of Postum (caffeine made her go all blotchy and hyperventilate) and a piece of the darkest chocolate she could find. Not a large piece. She could make a square or two last for her whole break, nibbling at the chocolate like a mouse.

Rosie picked up before the second ring. She sounded as if she was in midbite of chocolate.

"Rosie?"

"Karen? Are you still in England?"

"Of course I'm still here."

"I can't imagine it. What are you doing at this very moment?"

"Nothing exciting. Sitting in bed. But it's a very nice bed with very fluffy pillows and very crisp sheets."

"Oohh, sounds so British."

"I went to see *Macbeth* tonight."

"Was it gory?"

"A bit. Not bad. They played the ghost offstage."

"Hmm. Which means Macbeth was mad. Just as I suspected."

"I nearly fainted during the bloodstain scene," I confessed. "I think finding that dead man has taken a toll on me."

"Any more news on how he died?"

"Overdose of digitalis—but his wife claims that's

impossible, that she controlled the meds and he couldn't have taken too much."

"Did you fall down when you almost fainted?" Rosie asked.

"No, thank goodness, the man who owns the B and B I'm staying at was with me and he caught me."

"He went with you?"

"I had an extra ticket because of Dave."

"Poophead Dave. Forget about him. What is this man like?"

"Well, you know I told you about him. He runs a B and B and he cooks and he's extremely nice and everything here is perfectly neat and tidy."

"Sounds like a nice host." She cleared her throat. "How are his books?"

"That's the best part. He has an amazing library and I've only seen a small portion of it—just what's in my room."

"What does he look like?"

I thought of Caldwell, whose appearance was growing in my estimation. "Have you ever seen a hedgehog?"

"Just pictures."

"Well, he has that sort of look. Trim and tidy, with a hint of prickles."

"Sounds like you might like him."

"Maybe. Except this Frenchwoman waltzed in here tonight and kissed him on both cheeks."

"*Cherchez la femme,*" Rosie said.

I wondered if Rosie even knew she had just said, *Look for the woman.* She sometimes liked to throw in the odd French phrase just because she liked the way they sounded. "How are things going with Richard, your favorite patron? Has he been in to the library lately?"

"He's a fast reader. You know he took out three books two days ago and he was back in again today for three more."

"Well, that's a good sign. He must not have a girlfriend or he wouldn't be able to get that much reading done."

"I didn't quiz him on if he'd read them all. I didn't want to be rude."

"No, that was good."

"What should I do next, Karen?"

I stared out the window at the tops of the trees in Caldwell's garden. "I'm the last person who should be giving you advice on this subject. My track record is getting worse by the moment. All I can say is, be happy to see him, say his name, and always have a question ready to ask him."

"That sounds good. What question should I ask him?"

"Maybe who his favorite writer is."

"I think I can do that. I'll try it when he comes in next." She was quiet for a moment, then said, "Finished my chocolate. I'm glad you called. What are you going to do about the Frenchwoman?"

"Off with her head," I said.

TWENTY-ONE

❦

To Be Regular

When I came down the next morning Caldwell was putting the water on for tea. He didn't seem in the mood for a chat so I settled myself in the sitting room, waiting for him to bring in breakfast. I tried not to think about why he was being quiet. I thought he could at least thank me again for the evening at the theater.

As I sat there, hearing him thump around in the kitchen making me breakfast, I wondered if, after I left England, I would ever find someone like him in America. A man who knew how to take care of a woman. A man who read books. A man, period.

Maybe Dave would prove to be the last man in my life. What a horridly sour note to end on.

Sitting there musing on the possibilities of my future, I couldn't help but peruse the bookshelf of first editions. As my eyes wandered over the titles, I came upon *Winnie-the-Pooh,* the book Howard had been reading when he died. I was sorry he hadn't cared for the little bear, but knew he was not alone. Dorothy Parker, under her pseudonym Constant Reader, wrote a famous review of *The House at Pooh Corner,* a line of which read: "And it is that word 'hummy,' my darlings, that marks the first place in *The House at Pooh Corner* at which Tonstant Weader fwowed up."

I, however, loved all the Pooh books. Every time I read any of them, I chuckled all the way through.

I gently turned the pages of Caldwell's edition until I came upon some marginalia. Odd, but exciting. The phrase was written upside down. I turned the book around and read in a large and florid script: "Deadman's Balls."

The phrase certainly meant nothing to me. Could it possibly have been written by Howard? As he was dying? What an odd time to make note of that part of the male anatomy? Did he know what was happening to him and wanted to make remark on it?

Was he the deadman? Or had the notation already been there? Maybe he turned the book upside down to read the note. I'd have to check Howard's handwriting against the script.

I remembered the register Caldwell had me sign when I checked in. It was sitting in the hallway on a small table. I took the book and walked down to the register and turned back a page. There was Howard's signature: Howard and Annette Worth. I was no expert, but the slope of the writing was the same and the *d*'s were almost identical.

Next I turned to the front where Caldwell had written his name and address. I knew this was silly because Caldwell would never scribble anything in a first edition, but maybe he'd had the book since he was quite young and didn't know any better. But his handwriting was not at all similar to the writing in *Winnie-the-Pooh*.

As soon as I was back in the room, Caldwell entered, carrying a tray. I quickly shelved the book. I wasn't quite ready to ask him about the phrase and I wasn't sure why I was so hesitant. So I asked a different question.

"Caldwell, who's your favorite writer?" I might as well take my own advice and try to talk to him about something that I knew he loved.

"Seriously?" He didn't look as chipper as he normally did in the morning and was dressed quite informally in jeans and a sweatshirt. His hair was sticking up in back and his eyes looked larger and droopier than I remembered seeing them before. I had the odd impulse to reach out and smooth down his hair, pat him on the head, but I resisted.

I, on the other hand, was dressed smartly for the day and felt surprisingly rested. "I couldn't be more serious."

"Isn't it rather early in the day for 'serious'?"

I didn't want to know why he was barely awake. I hated the thought of how late he might have stayed up with Francine, drinking wine and who knew what else they might have been doing.

"Do you mean you have to think about it?" I asked.

"Yes, but before I answer your question, I must thank you for a lovely evening. I have missed the theater. Don't really like to go alone. Not the same at all." He poured himself a cup of tea and stood, looking down at me. "Back to your question. Do you remember what you said to me yesterday when I asked which of Shakespeare's plays was your favorite tragedy?"

"Yes, of course I remember."

"Well, it's the same for me. It changes depending on the day. And I'm not sure what kind of day this is. If it's a Graham Greene day or a Jane Austen day. It might even be a John Fowles day."

"Really? John Fowles. He is a terrific writer, isn't he?" I reread *Daniel Martin* about once every three years. I loved the sense he gave in that book of the possibilities in life never closing down, that even in the darkest moments love might appear. I didn't dare ask Caldwell what his favorite Fowles book was—if he said *The Collector*, I might not like him as much.

He pulled out a chair across from me and sank into it. "So, Miss Bright and Cheerful, who is your favorite author?"

"Fowles is right up there, but I find him uneven. I'd have to say Harper Lee."

"But she only wrote one book."

"But it was a perfect book."

We both heard footsteps on the stairway and turned to see Francine slink into the room.

Unlike myself and Caldwell, she was still in her nightclothes, and what magnificent clothes they were: a lovely, off-white silk robe tied around her waist, with a froth of lace from her nightgown showing at the wrists and throat. Loose, her dark hair waved over her shoulders.

But her eyes didn't look good—they were sunken and smudged, giving the impression that they were receding into her head. Without any makeup, her face was washed out, a look that was either tuber-culous or vampiristic—either way, not particularly attractive.

"Oh, the night, she was terrible," she said.

I took her voicing this comment to both of us as a sign that Caldwell had not been privy to her night, which gave me a slight rush of gladness.

"I'm sorry to hear that," I responded, trying to keep the joy out of my voice.

"I told you not to open that second bottle of wine. I hope you didn't drink all of it." Without wait-ing for an answer, Caldwell asked, "Francine, how many shots of coffee do you want this morning?"

She sank into his now empty chair and put a hand to her head. *"Beaucoup, s'il te plaît."*

"How about three?"

"That will do for the beginning."

When he left us, she tilted forward and put her forehead on the table. There was an awkward si-lence.

Finally I lifted up the rack of toast. "Would you like some toast? Sometimes eating helps."

Her head came up slowly and she looked at me as if she had forgotten I even existed. She shook her head at my offer. "You must forgive me. I drank like the fish last night. Sometimes it happens."

"I know what you mean," I said. "The first night I was here . . . You know, this is my first time in London—actually it's my first time on this side of the pond. Well, I didn't know how big a pint was and I drank a few. Too many. I felt awful the next day. I know what you mean." I stopped myself from saying any more. It was quite unlike me to ramble on in this manner.

"Never before in Europe?" She squinched her nose.

"Never."

"But surely you've been to France."

"Not even France." I asked, "Have you been to the States?"

"But of course. New York, the Miami Beach, Boston. One must travel to see the world."

"Well, I'm from the middle of the country and everything is a lot farther from there." I thought about Sunshine Valley for a moment and had a tweak of homesickness. "Do you come to London often?"

At that moment Caldwell carried in a tray with a small cup of very black coffee and a plate with only a piece of dry toast on it. I looked at the toast and then at the large slab of butter.

Francine noticed my glance. "The regime," she said, patting her belly, or the area where a belly would have been if she'd had one.

The older I got the less interested I was in going on a diet. I was enjoying eating more than ever and I wasn't about to give it up so I would live a few more months, right at the end of my life, when nothing would taste good anyway.

With that in mind, I reached out for a second piece of toast and set it down in the midst of the crumbs on my plate. I slathered butter on it and, after I had eaten the first bite, said to Caldwell, "Good bread."

"I bought it yesterday."

"I think day-old bread toasts better."

Suddenly a tromping came from upstairs as two pairs of feet hit the stairs and two loud voices pondered the weather. Francine looked up in alarm. I wondered if she had met the Tweedles before. *This should be fun,* I thought.

They came through the doorway at the same time, but stopped when they saw Francine. They were both wearing white blouses and scarves in the style of the Boy Scouts, one green and one gold, neither good colors on the ruddy women. Blue polyester pants completed their ensembles. But one of them had a sweater over her arm and the other had a raincoat.

"Oh, we have more company," the gold Tweedle said, holding her hands in front of her chest as if she had captured a bird.

I determined to learn their names and find some physical characteristic I could link to each of them.

"But you're not even dressed," the green Tweedle said as she sucked in her breath. "Can you do that at a B and B?"

"She has a bathrobe on. Like in Georgette Heyer novels when the women put on a morning gown," said gold Tweedle.

Francine was staring at them, her mouth held in a tight line. In comparison to the robust Tweedles, she looked even more pallid. I immediately liked the Tweedles more than ever. It was time to introduce them.

"This is Francine," I said and then waved at the two women, saying, "This is Betty and Barb."

"I'm Betty," the one wearing the gold scarf said. I scanned her broad face and saw she had a mole by her left eye.

"And I'm Barb. We're both from Omaha."

Francine continued to look stunned.

"That's in Nebraska," Betty explained.

Francine turned to me. "Nebraska?"

"That's probably someplace you haven't visited. The middle of the country," I told her gently. "Francine is from France."

They both hovered over us, clapping their hands. "Oh, this is wonderful. A real Frenchwoman."

Barb leaned close to Francine and said very loudly, "We're very happy to meet you. Our first real French person."

"Practice your French, Barb," Betty said.

"On chant tea," Barb said.

Francine looked at me. Somehow I had become the translator. "I think she's saying, 'enchanted.'"

"Does she know about Howard?" Betty asked.

"I'm sure Caldwell told her," I answered.

"It's made everything so different, him not being here," Barb said, starting to pull out a handkerchief.

"My head, it is hurt," Francine said, waving her hand as if to distract them. "Oh-la-la. I have a very badness here."

"Oh, no. Did you fall down?" Betty asked. Then, as an aside to Barb, she said in a loud whisper, "Did you notice—she actually said oh-la-la, just like in the movies. Isn't that something?"

Caldwell came bustling in with two big bowls of what appeared to be oatmeal. Betty and Barb sat down next to each other on the love seat and he set the bowls in front of them. They each poured a healthy dollop of milk over the cereal and then sprinkled the tops with brown sugar.

"We love the coarse-ground oatmeal. It's from Scotland. Caldwell gets it in special for us. It keeps us going all day long," Barb said. "He calls it porridge. Isn't that cute? Like Goldilocks and the Three Bears."

"And it keeps us regular," Betty added.

"Regular?" Francine looked at me.

I really didn't want to go there. "Satisfied," I explained.

Francine nodded, then stared at the two women eating their oats. "I must go to my room. Nice to meet you." She stood with her cup of coffee clutched in her hands and left the room.

"She looks a little peaky to me," Barb said.

"Remember that book about French women? How they never get fat? How they drink wine with every meal? I think she's taken it too far. She's way too skinny and I'd say it looks like she had a little too much of the vino last night," Betty said, nudging Barb with her elbow. They both tittered.

The women from Omaha again went up in my estimation.

"Karen is at least as elegant as that woman, even if Francine is French. And she's a good healthy weight. Much more sensible." Barb acted as if I couldn't hear what she was saying.

As if to remind her that I was sitting right there, Betty turned her attention to me and asked, "Did

you have a good time with our Caldwell last night?
We didn't even hear you come in. But then we sleep
like logs."

"Yes, I had a nice time."

"And how was the play, Karen?"

"Bloody unforgettable," I said.

TWENTY-TWO

Raise a Ruckus

One dead man on my trip was enough. I decided to take the bull by the horns and go tell Dave about the man I might have accidentally sicced on him. Much as I never wanted to see Dave again, I owed him that. The good news was that Honey knew the man I was talking about—she had been conversing with him at the National Gallery—so she could be on the lookout for him. I don't know what I thought Guy would do, but I didn't want to have to worry about it anymore.

Walking in London was like going to a most ex-

clusive museum—a slice of history on every street—
and it was free. I put on my walking shoes and
hoped that Madame Frou-Frou wouldn't see me
in them. I didn't understand why sports shoes for
women had to be so unattractive. Neon lime green
really didn't go with anything in my wardrobe, but
back home they had looked fine.

When I came down the stairs I overheard
Caldwell and Francine talking in the hallway and
stopped midflight, not wanting to interrupt them.

"I have to finish up some work here," Caldwell
told her. "I'll meet you for lunch later."

"Very good," she said. "Let's try that new bistro by
the Tate. It seems very sympa. Ciao."

I heard what I hoped were air kisses, a set of two.

After the sound of the front door closing I descended the stairs. They were a couple. *Tant pis,*
I thought. Really too bad. Only because I thought
that Caldwell deserved better than that tightly
strung woman. This thought led me to wonder, as
I did often these days, whether I would ever have
another man in my life.

When I walked down the hallway, Caldwell had
gone into the kitchen. I popped my head in. "I'm off
for the day."

He was cleaning up the breakfast dishes. There
was a moment when I thought of offering to help,

but that gesture felt wrong. After all, I was paying him to lodge me. Maybe I shouldn't have invited him to *Macbeth*. Maybe he had gone because I was his guest and he didn't feel like he could say no to me. Suddenly I realized I didn't understand the rules in this country.

Caldwell looked up, with his hands in soapy water, and smiled a wan smile. "Have a good day," he said.

Walking to the Queen's Arms Hotel took longer than I had thought it would and I heard a clock tower strike twelve as I finally found the right street. I had taken a few wrong turns—as good as I was at finding my way, this city stymied me with its curving, narrow streets that weren't on a grid.

As I walked along, I took the time to go over what I knew about Howard's death. While the police were treating it as accidental, several things were making me think it wasn't. Annette seemed so sure that she wouldn't have given him an overdose of his digitalis—although there was always the possibility, as the Tweedles seemed to think, that she might have done it on purpose, to get his money. And she seemed fed up with the life she'd been leading with him.

The Tweedles both seemed so fond of him and

I could think of no reason why they would want him dead—but they had been there that night and couldn't be ruled out.

Then there was Caldwell. Little as I wanted to think it, he had both opportunity and motive. He could easily have gone into their room and taken a dose of digitalis. But how would he have given it to Howard? Also, he had reason to dislike Howard. But to kill him? After this much time? It just didn't make sense.

And I didn't want it to be true.

As I approached the entrance to the hotel, I told myself to leave Howard Worth's death alone. Right now I needed to take care of Dave so I wouldn't have his nonaccidental death on my mind.

A tall, thin-lipped concierge was standing behind the desk and looked me up and down as I approached him. I was sure he did not miss my shoes and pegged me as an American immediately.

"Hello, good morning," I said.

"Good afternoon," he corrected. "May I help you?"

"Yes, I believe a Mr. Dave Richter is staying here," I started to say.

At the mention of Dave's name, he interrupted me. "I'm sorry to say that Mr. Richter is no longer with us."

"No longer with us," I repeated. My stomach lurched. That sounded rather ominous. Could Guy have done something to Dave already before I had a chance to stop him? "What happened to him?"

The concierge shrugged. "One must be discreet about such things, but in point of fact it was all because of his traveling companion."

"What did she have to do with it?"

The concierge tightened his eyes and screwed up his mouth, but I could see that the words were pushing against his teeth. He had been dying to tell someone. He leaned over and said in a very loud whisper, "She wanted to be served dinner in the middle of the night. Two o'clock in the morning, to be exact. She raised what I believe you would call a ruckus."

I was confused. "A ruckus? What happened?"

"I wasn't here, but the story I was told was that she tried to go into the kitchen herself and take some food."

"Oh."

"And wine."

"Oh, I see." Her behavior did sound inappropriate.

"I believe she had already consumed too much alcohol."

"Yes, quite."

"After some force, she was dissuaded from doing

that. I have reason to believe she was not happy."

"And Dave?"

"I think Mr. Richter slept through most of this intemperate scene. But they left the next day. That was yesterday."

"They left?"

"Yes, as I said, they are no longer with us."

"Oh, that's what you meant. I wasn't sure. I thought maybe something bad had happened to Dave."

The concierge stared at me for a moment before saying, "He is traveling with that woman. That seems punishment enough."

I couldn't have agreed more. "Do you know where they went?"

"As they did not pay for all their charges, I doubt we will be hearing from them again. They gave no indication as to where they might be found."

"Oh," I said, then thought maybe it was just as well. If I couldn't find them, then hopefully Guy couldn't either.

I walked into the first café I came across and ordered a bowl of soup. I pulled my what-to-do-in-England list out of my pocket and stared at it. Museums, gardens, castles, more museums. I put the list down and stared out the window.

I found it odd how I vacillated between feeling revved up and excited about really being in England, and feeling somewhat lethargic and completely out of place.

Being with Dave in London would have been a struggle. I knew that. He wouldn't have wanted to do everything I wanted to do. He would have been crabby in the morning. He would have wanted to go to a pub every night, watch TV in our room, and complain when there was no football on.

But he would have provided a bit of insulation for me. He would have been more out of place than me in this cosmopolitan city, and so I would have felt more comfortable. Even though I would never have done what Honey did—demand food in the middle of the night—I rather liked her spirit for doing it.

I found myself working so hard to fit in that I often didn't enjoy myself very much. Maybe it was time to relax and be an American, lime-green walking shoes and all. Not try to speak with a British accent, not try to do everything on my list, not try to figure out what was going on with Caldwell, and certainly not try to compete with Madame Frou-Frou.

A big bowl of mulligatawny soup was placed in front of me. It tasted of faraway spices in a delectable broth. My mother had made soup similar to this and called it *slumgullion,* a combination of everything that was left in the fridge.

When I was done, the waitress came up and asked, "Would you care for something sweet?"

That was exactly what I wanted—a sweet. "Yes, please. What do you have?"

"Spotted dick and a trifle."

As much as I wanted to order a dish named "spotted dick," I took the safe route and ordered a sweet I was both more familiar with and knew from past experience that I would love. "I'll have the trifle."

When the trifle came—layers of cake and pudding and fruit covered with whipped cream—I contemplated it for a while. A small temple to all sweet things. All my life I had loved pudding. I remember my mother saying that she liked to chew her food herself, but I enjoyed the feeling of licking the creamy froth off my spoon. I ate the whole thing, scraping the side of the bowl with my spoon. My promise to not count calories on this trip was proving to be a most excellent decision.

Thus fortified, I decided to give myself the biggest challenge of all.

I would simply wander for the rest of the day, to truly be in London, expecting nothing, with no place to go, nothing I had to see. I would walk down one street and decide which way to turn. For someone who always has a plan, who always follows a map, who always knows what time it is, this was a difficult task—to let go of all expectations and take the world as it came.

And so I did. For the rest of the afternoon, I stopped in shops when I felt like it, I smelled fruit, I sat in comfy chairs, I looked at artwork. In short, I strolled through the streets of London like I owned them.

Turning down one narrow street, I came upon a small bookstore called "Paul Haddington Antiquarian Bookseller." The perfume of old books—leather, dust, leaves—hit me as I walked into the small space. The store was so narrow that it was actually taller than it was wide. Shelves covered the walls up to the ceiling and there was a ladder that you could push around and climb to reach the top. I was not exactly a collector, but I always had a list of books that I would like to add to my personal library, books that for whatever reason held a particular charm for me.

One was Dickens's *The Pickwick Papers,* which I had read for the first time in sixth grade. I remembered clearly sitting in the school library and feeling as if I was living in a different time and a different place. That book was probably the real reason that I was attracted to all things English. After that, I had come to dearly love Dickens's work and was close to having a complete set of older editions.

There, on a waist-high shelf tucked in next to *A Tale of Two Cities,* was a small leather-bound book titled *The Posthumous Papers of the Pickwick Club.* I had found it.

I carefully extracted the volume from the shelf, opened it, and saw with delight that it was also illustrated. While the *Papers* had been originally published in the 1830s as pamphlets, the book I was holding had been published a hundred years later. Still, it might be worth something. Plus, more important, I liked it.

When I turned to read the price written on the inside cover in pencil, I saw that it was nearly out of my range: $350. I gulped but pulled out my credit card to buy it. A gift to myself.

"Where'd you find this?" the store clerk asked. He looked like he was about twelve years old and as if he had combed his thick black hair with a corkscrew.

"Right with all the rest of Dickens."

"Must have come in recently. Nice book, this. Did you know that when the *Pickwick Papers* were originally published they were serialized, coming out once a month for twenty months?"

"Yes, I do happen to know that and that the last serial was a double issue, which broke records for its sales."

The boy's face fell as he wrapped up the book and I wished I could take my know-it-all comment back, but it was hard sometimes to squelch the librarian. "You seem to know his work quite well. What's your favorite Dickens?" I asked.

"Oh, it has to be *David Copperfield*. My own life story right there. Like David I've come to London to find my fortune." He smiled from beneath his dark bangs and I wished him well.

As my feet were threatening to turn into bloody stumps, I sat down outside the bookseller and pulled out a map to figure out where I was. I had walked for hours, but had actually not gone too far. Fortunately I was close to a tube stop.

Since it was rush hour the car was crowded, but in my new mood, I enjoyed it, the crush of people from all over the world, men wearing turbans, young girls with pierced eyebrows, an old woman carrying her older toy poodle, who was wearing a pair of sunglasses (the dog, not the woman), the dignified British businessmen in their dark suits.

One of the things about everyone looking different is that it starts to not matter anymore. People become just people, not representative of any country or race. No one gave me more than my fair share of glances. They probably thought, *American tourist wearing comfortable, ugly shoes.*

When I came out of the tube station, the woman in front of me pulled out her cell phone and checked it. An automatic response caused me to copy her. There weren't many people who knew my number, but there was one message. Maybe Rosie had called with news on her romance.

When I checked the message, I heard a slightly familiar British male voice say, "They moved camp, but I managed to track them down. Don't worry about the plumber. I've got the situation well in hand."

TWENTY-THREE

~~~

Why Hay-on-Wye?

I stood on the top step of Caldwell's house, puzzled and worried. The voice had been Guy's, of that I was sure. Also, he was the only man in England who might have my cell phone number.

When I tried to get Guy's number all that showed up on my phone was a bunch of zeroes, probably because it was an international phone number. How had he gotten my number without comprehending my message? Had I been unclear? What did he mean, he was taking care of the situation?

Guy sounded like he was still messing around

about Dave. Now the situation was even worse. I didn't know where Dave was, but Guy did. I was rocking back and forth on the front steps, when the door flew open and Caldwell looked out at me. "Hello," he said.

"Hi," I said back.

"Good day?" he asked.

"Not bad," I said, not wanting to say anything more.

"Coming in?"

"Sure."

He stepped back and peered at the book I was carrying. I had unwrapped it to look at it on the tube. "What do you have there?"

"A book," I said.

"Looks oldish," he said.

I handed it to him. He took it reverently. "Dickens. *Pickwick Papers*. Oh, yes, this is splendid." He gently turned to the copyright page. "Obviously not a first edition, but still worth some money I think. Where did you find it?"

"Not too far from here." I told him the name of the shop. "I wasn't really looking for anything—just browsing."

"How much did you pay for it?"

Rather embarrassed at how much I had paid, I hesitated, then told him.

He flared his nostrils and patted the book. "You're a good browser. I'd say that this little beauty is worth nearly ten times that much."

"Seriously. Or are you funning me?"

"Why would I do that? Hang on to it. I think Dickens is due a revival and it will only go up in value." He handed me back the book with reluctance. "Do you often buy old books?"

I thought of the hoards of books lining all the rooms of my house and reminded myself not to slip into librarian mode. "Only if I like the book. So, sometimes. I have a few odds and ends. You seem to collect books too."

"Well, I'm going to Hay-on-Wye later on this week. Have you heard of this town?" he asked.

Hay-on-Wye. A small town located on the border of England and Wales with at least thirty antiquarian bookstores. Mecca to book collectors. I was dying to go there. When I had planned the trip with Dave I hadn't dared suggest we go to Hay-on-Wye. I knew Dave would have died of boredom.

I squeaked out, "Yes. More bookstores than any other small town in England."

"It's about two hundred miles from London."

One hundred and seventy-nine miles, if I remembered correctly. "How long will that take you?"

"Oh, I'll leave early. I like to get there as the

shops open and then spend the day." He lifted his eyes up. "I would be gone for the whole day. I feel the need for some new books. Howard's death has been such a disturbance. I need to do something to cheer myself up. Don't you think?"

He was asking me to approve his reason for going on this long-awaited trip. "Absolutely. Cheering up is always good."

"You wouldn't care to go along, would you?"

I noticed that he put the question in the negative, but I jumped on it. "Yes, I would love that."

"You wouldn't mind being gone so long from London in the middle of your trip and all?" Again, a question.

"There is nothing I would rather do."

"Fine then. Let's say in two days we'll go."

When Caldwell smiled, I was relieved. I could tell he did want me to go.

Francine walked in from the sitting room. "Where are we going?" she asked.

"Karen and I are going to Hay-on-Wye," he told her.

"I will go also," she said as she slipped her hand onto his arm.

"But the whole town is filled with books, in English," Caldwell said, pointing out, "You don't read, and especially not in English."

"I'm sure there will be other things to do."

He cleared his throat. "I thought you were going back to Paris?"

She slitted her eyes like a cat. "It can wait until the weekend. I wouldn't want to miss this voyage."

I curled up on my bed with my new old book, on which Mr. Pickwick looked very pompous with his walking stick and waistcoat bulging at the buttons. I must admit I was handling it more carefully now that I had learned how much the volume was worth. This discovery made me wonder about some of the other older books I had picked up in my years of amateur collecting. I had never checked out how much any of them would be worth, I just paid what I could afford for what I liked. That way I was never disappointed.

Then I thought of the millions of books I would be perusing in a couple days. Going to Hay-on-Wye with Caldwell would be a dream come true, even with Madame F-F coming along. For the chance to wander through miles of books, I would not let that French fatal femme get in my way.

Just as I was thinking about what to do about Dave, the phone rang. I scrambled off the bed. I could hear my cell but not find it. It must have been in my purse but I couldn't find that either. Maybe it would be Guy and I could find out what he thought he was doing. I had to find that phone.

On the fourth ring I thought to look under the bed and dug it out of my purse. I slammed the phone to my ear and said, "Hello?"

"Inopportune moment?" Rosie asked. "Were you in the tub?"

"Long day. Couldn't find my phone."

"Say no more. Guess what, guess what?"

I could picture Rosie jiggling up and down as she talked. I would not ruin her pleasure of telling me by guessing that something momentous had happened in her ongoing quest of the sci-fi guy.

"What?" I asked.

"We're going to see a movie together. Richard and I."

"Great!" I said. "You're going on a date?"

"Well, I'm not sure if it's a date. You see, I did what you told me to do. I asked him who his favorite author was. Gene Wolfe, whom I barely have read. But we got talking more and somehow I mentioned Jules Verne and he said that this funky movie theater by the university was playing *Journey to the Center of the Earth*, and we both started laughing and thought wouldn't that be weird to go see it and then we kind of decided to go see it and we thought we might as well go together since we were both going to go see it and I guess it might be a date."

"Act as if it is."

"Oh," Rosie said. "How do I do that?"

"Dress up. Wear lipstick. Smile at him. Be sure and go out for drinks afterward. Flirt."

"Yeah. Flirt. I might have to take out a book on that. I don't really know how to do that."

I knew what she meant. I had had to bone up on flirting when I was her age. I still wasn't very good at it. "Tilt your head when he talks. Touch his arm. Flip your hair back over your shoulder."

"My hair's about two inches long."

"Doesn't work then."

"How's it going with you? How's the Frenchwoman? She still alive?"

"Yes, she is, and butting into everything. But the main thing I'm worried about is Dave."

"What?" she said. "How can you stand to think about him after what he did to you?"

So I explained about how I had blathered away to a strange man in a pub who had some kind of connections in the criminal world about how Dave had done me wrong and then I had seen this same man talking to Honey. Then how I had tried to warn Dave but he had left his hotel and I couldn't find him.

"I don't know what to do," I finished.

Rosie said, "You have to find him. If he dies, it will ruin your trip. Think. Where would an American plumber go in London?"

TWENTY-FOUR

Holiday, Anyone?

In the middle of the night, I woke and couldn't get back to sleep. Nightmares of missed planes, sleeping men falling over dead, and geese running at me with slashing beaks had plagued me. I don't know what Freud would have made of these images, but I understood what they were telling me: I was afraid I had set something in motion that I was unable to stop.

As Rosie put it, much would be ruined if something bad happened to Dave. Plus, I had a few other things I had been rehearsing saying to Dave on how he had treated me.

Unable to settle down, I crawled out of bed and sat down in front of Caldwell's bookshelf. My eyes wandered down the rows of books, looking for anomalies. I liked books to be organized, not just by author, but also alphabetically, by name of book. Arranging books always calmed me down. Taking control of something and putting it in the proper order made me feel like I had some actual power in the world. I started moving books around and hoped Caldwell wouldn't notice that I had messed with his library. Or if he noticed, that he would be pleased.

Dave's toadlike head kept appearing in front of the books, rather like the pretend Wizard of Oz against the velvet curtains. The persistence of this vision told me I had much unfinished business with him.

I thought back to our travels together. Dave was the kind of guy who liked familiarity. In a flash it hit me where he might be and I couldn't believe I hadn't thought of it earlier. I dropped the book I had in my hand and stood up. Reaching into the drawer of the bedside table, I found the enormous London yellow pages.

Even browsing through a phone directory made me happy, especially the yellow pages. Everything organized in categories was reassuring and somehow satisfying.

I turned to the hotel section and found the middle of the alphabet. There were five Holiday Inns in London. I could call them tomorrow and find out if Dave was staying at one of them.

When we had traveled in the States, Dave loved staying at Holiday Inns. He had always been impressed by the plumbing, I guess. He had not been happy about the idea of a bed-and-breakfast when I had made the reservation. He said he didn't want to have to eat breakfast with anyone he didn't know.

I climbed back in bed and easily fell back to sleep, having a strong sense that I would be able to track him down and finally rid him from my life. The floating head of Dave wavered in my dream, then popped like a big balloon.

The next morning, before I ventured downstairs, I called all the Holiday Inns. I would find Dave, warn him, and then do what I planned to do today—go to the Chelsea Flower Show to see Annette Worth receive Howard's award.

I had almost given up hope of finding Dave when the young woman who answered the phone at the second to last one said yes, a Mr. Dave Richter was staying with them. She asked if she should ring through to his room.

"No, I'd like to surprise him."

"Lovely," she said.

Two hours later I was standing outside the Holiday Inn, a gleaming white and silver building with a big green *H* cutting across the front of it like a brand on a horse's flank. In no way did this structure resemble what one would think of as a quaint, quintessential London hotel. There was a Starbucks right next door. If I didn't know I was in England, I would have guessed anyplace America. Sad that places had become so interchangeable. Why travel if it was all the same?

I walked into the lobby and was impressed by how spacious it felt: The ceiling went up at least three stories, the lounge chairs were large enough to fit two people, and the Persian rug was the size of a basketball court. This bigger-than-life sensation made me realize that most rooms in England—unless they were in palaces—were smaller than rooms in the States. I noticed that the British people walked with shorter steps. There was a slightly squished feeling to most restaurants and cafés, tables closer together than I was used to.

At the same time, it felt good to have a little more room around me, and yet I was disappointed to find this American hotel in the midst of London.

Odd how two conflicting feelings can coexist in our brains.

I forced myself to go to the lobby phone and call Dave's room. The operator put me through. After the phone buzzed twice, a woman's voice answered, sounding quite sleepy, "Hello?"

I said nothing. Honey sounded about fifteen years old and slightly cranky. I could imagine her rubbing her eyes.

Why did it have to hit me again and again that Dave had dumped me and taken up with a young woman, young enough that I could, in fact, be her mother? Each time the thought of it sank in, it went a little deeper into my psyche and the air rushed out of my gut as if I'd been punched.

"Who's this?" Honey asked.

I had no intention of speaking. I simply wanted to know if they were there, in the hotel.

"We didn't ask for a wake-up call." The phone was slammed down at the other end.

I walked back out to the lobby to wait. I did not want to go up to their room. It would simply be too painful to get a glimpse of their shared bed. Plus, there was less likely to be a scene out in public. Or so I'd thought.

For over an hour I sat, facing the elevators, and watched the streams of people flowing in and out

of the hotel. Again, the variety of faces from all over
the world was stunning to me. I became so caught
up in guessing what countries different people were
from that I almost forgot why I was sitting there.

The elevator doors opened and Dave stepped out
with Honey right behind him. He looked rumpled
and blurry-eyed in faded khakis and a Twins sweatshirt while she looked perky and ready for the day
in skintight jeans and two layers of T-shirts, her hair
pulled up in a ponytail as tight as her jeans.

I felt a rage inside myself pushing upward. He
wasn't good enough to have left me. How had that
happened? I tried to calm myself down by wrapping
my hands together and holding on.

Taking deep breaths, I let them get into the middle of the room before I approached them.

"Dave," I said to stop them.

He turned. "Karen?" He took a step backward.

Honey stood next to Dave, looking puzzled.

"I have to talk to you." Emotions were swamping
me. A fierce and rare form of anger was bubbling up
from deep inside me, something I had never felt before.

Seeing Honey up close again made me realize
that she wasn't that bad looking, thin and a little
wispy, but lovely skin and big brown eyes, which
made me angrier than ever.

"Who is this?" she asked Dave.

"Dave, you might be in danger. I can explain."

Dave looked gobsmacked, a terrific Irish word that I had never had the opportunity to use. "How did you get here, Karen? My God, did you follow us all the way to England?"

"Listen, it's a long story, but I have to warn you," I started.

Honey grabbed Dave's arm and asked again, "Who is this woman?"

"You want to know who I am?" I said, my voice rising in my throat. "I'm the woman whose place you took. I'm the woman who made the money for this trip possible. I'm the woman who should be standing next to Dave. This was my trip. Mine."

"What are you talking about?" Honey said as she nervously looked over at Dave.

"I'm Dave's girlfriend." I refused to use the words *old* or *ex*. "Didn't he tell you about me?"

"Since when?"

"For about four years until five days ago."

Honey's big brown eyes grew larger, then slitted down as she turned to Dave. In a loud-mouthy voice, she said, "You had a girlfriend? When we met you said you weren't seeing anyone."

Dave looked as if he had just eaten something rotten.

People turned to stare at us. The librarian in me came out. "Please lower your voice," I said to Honey. I turned to Dave. All the words I had been storing up since he had dumped me came crowding forward, all the imaginary conversations I had had with him, all the questions I wanted to ask. "How could you treat me the way you did? After four years? After the Flush Budget? After all our plans for this trip? Why did you do that?"

Dave shrugged, lifted up his hands and said, "It just happened. She sat down next to me."

"Hey, buddy, you came on to me. You bought me a drink. I was just sitting there minding my own business," Honey reminded him. "Don't make it sound like I went after you."

I almost felt sorry for him. Honey seemed genuinely angry—but not as angry as I was. "Well, get used to it, *honey*. Coming here to England without him is the best thing he never did for me. I'm having the time of my life. I'm going to Hay-on-Wye, I'm seeing Shakespeare plays, I'm buying beautiful clothes, going into bookstores, doing everything I want to do. Dave would have been a drag."

At my outburst, Honey grabbed Dave's arm and shook it. "I would never have given you the time of day if I had known you were involved. But what I hate the most is that you lied. How can I ever trust you?"

"You can't," I told her.

Dave's eyes shifted back and forth. I could see that he was still having trouble taking in the sight of the two sides of his life colliding. Pathetic man. I had to get out of there before I strangled him. "Look, the only reason I'm here—and I don't know why I bothered—is someone might be trying to kill you."

Impossibly, Dave looked even more stunned. He sputtered, "Kill me?"

Honey started laughing at me. "Wow. You are kind of nuts. What are you talking about? Have you lost it?"

"I have lost nothing." I had come to the hard part of what I had to do—confess to my role in this mess. "And it's my fault because I talked to someone about what you did to me, dumping me and all. I told this guy that I wanted to kill you. I wasn't serious, but I suppose he could have thought I was. Little did I know at the time that he was involved with criminal elements. I'm really not sure what he might do. But it was a mistake, a misunderstanding."

Dave shook his head. "Karen, I don't know what you're talking about and I don't want to know. Please leave Kirstin and me alone."

"If you don't believe me, ask her." I pointed at Kirstin, not wanting to say her name. "She knows the man who might be after you."

"What are you talking about? What man?" Kirstin asked.

"At the National Gallery. Remember when you were standing outside? I saw you talking with him—a tall blond guy."

At this, she paused and I swore I saw comprehension cross her face. She shook her head, her blond ponytail switching back and forth. "What guy? I don't know what you're talking about. I didn't talk to anyone anyplace. You're making this all up. Stupid cow!"

After calling me a bovine creature, she lunged straight at me, both hands slamming into my shoulders with surprising force. I pitched backward and landed on my butt on the Persian rug.

Stunned and embarrassed, I sat there and watched the two of them stalk out of the lobby.

A bellboy with a dark complexion and doelike eyes came and stood over me, offering me a hand.

"May I help you, Madame?" he asked.

I let him pull me up and dust me off while I murmured, "Thank you, but I think I'm past help."

TWENTY-FIVE

A Rose by Any Other Name

I wandered down the paths at the Chelsea Flower Show until my feet were too tired to walk any farther. I sat on a bench to take in the oddly bucolic city scene. Clouds were languidly lolling through the light blue sky, their shapes reflecting in the water of the pond of the National Press Club garden. An opening in the trees on the horizon pulled the eye into the distance. Such a sense of space and vistas right in the middle of London.

There were no straight lines in this landscape; rather, the gravel walk curved around the pond, following the contours of the land. I knew it was due to the influence of Lancelot "Capability" Brown and his theory of the "Line of Grace." He had been the surveyor of the royal gardens. He believed in what he called "placemaking" and thought that there should be no rigid directions, no straight lines.

Capability Brown was right. I could see that now. There were no straight lines in the whole wide world. I desperately wanted there to be a straight line between a problem and its solution. But since Dave had dumped me I felt like I was meandering around in a world I no longer recognized.

I didn't seem to know what love was; I didn't understand why he hadn't wanted to be with me anymore; I'd set something in motion that I couldn't stop; an old man had died reading a book upside down. Everything seemed out of control. And yet here I was in this beautiful place, on a perfect day, paths curving away in all inviting directions. What more could one want?

I had that dizzying, horrible feeling that one gets after spinning around in circles until they were almost sick—elated and nauseous at the same time.

A mighty stand of foxglove pulled me toward it and I stepped off the path to lean in closer to the flowers and take a sniff.

I heard a voice behind me say, "Resist."

I turned and found a tall youngish man in a striped shirt looking at me. He was smiling. I smiled back.

"Why?" I asked.

"It might kill you."

"Sniffing a foxglove?"

"Yes. They are a very dangerous plant, especially the top leaves, and I read—mind you, I don't know if you can believe all you read—but I read in an old herbalist that even a deep breath from a foxglove could be enough to send someone into cardiac arrest."

"Digitalis," I remembered. "Of course."

"Yes, that one is digitalis . . . I think. Not my specialty."

I stepped back onto the path and found he was a good head taller than me. "So you have saved my life."

He leaned over me. "Oh, you're American."

"Yes."

"On holiday?" he asked.

Holiday had such a nicer sound than vacation. "Yes," I admitted. "My first time here."

"How're you liking our fair country?"

"Very much, thank you."

"Good, because you see, I am responsible for your happiness," he said, pointing to his chest.

For a splendid moment, I thought he really meant it, that he would take responsibility for me and my stay here in England, that he wanted to make sure I had a good time. "Oh, how does that happen?"

"I work for the British Tourist Authority," he said. "The RHS Chelsea Flower Show is our first big draw in the spring."

"Well, it's nice to be able to thank you in person."

We both laughed, after which a slight silence fell.

"Andrew Chumley," he introduced himself.

"Karen Nash," I said, shaking his hand. I looked him over. What I liked about him best was his crooked smile; one side of his mouth lifted up higher, and it gave him a bit of a snarly look.

Up close I could see that Andrew also had the crinkle lines around his eyes that I found attractive. When I was much younger, in my twenties, I did not find older men attractive and I was worried about what I would do when I myself was older. But now when I looked at men in their twenties, they just looked like unformed landscapes to me—their faces were bland, blank, showing no sense of character. I loved to look at older men's faces.

"Karen, if I may ask, how do you find the show?" he asked.

"Less British than I might have expected. I thought there'd be more formal gardens and then country gardens. Lots of this is just too modern for me."

"Ah, a traditionalist," he surmised.

"Maybe I am. I never thought of it that way."

"And what brought you to the show?"

"Literally or figuratively?"

"Figuratively," he acknowledged my question.

"I know someone who is getting an award for a rose they made."

He tilted his head. "Who is that?"

"Well, he was. He's not anymore. Howard Worth."

"Oh, yes. The Rosa 'Almost Blue Annette,' stunningly voluptuous. What happened to Mr. Worth?"

"Well, he died recently."

"I'm sorry to hear that. But he was getting on."

"Not so on. He was only seventy and seemed quite full of energy."

"He certainly kept busy. I think this is his third new rose in the last five years," he said.

"Did you know him?"

"Only a bit. I'm a rose man myself."

"Did you know his wife, Annette?"

"We just met a couple days ago. I guess she's not much for flowers. They seemed an odd pair to me."

"How much is this prize that he's getting for the rose?" I asked, wondering if money could have played a role in his death.

"Oh, the prize money is minimal; it's the exposure and the market with this new hybrid. Everyone's been trying to make a blue rose. It's like the holy grail of the hybridization nutties. Howard maybe has come as close as is possible. Although, if he were still alive, who knows what he might have produced."

"So it's worth a lot."

"You could say." He fell silent for a moment, then asked, "So what have you done on your trip thus far?"

I told him my list: the National Gallery, the Globe, walking along the Thames, wandering into bookstores.

"Bookshops, we call them here." He popped himself in the mouth. "Sorry, bad habit of mine, correcting people's English."

"Not at all. I love to be corrected. I'm fascinated by the differences in our two languages. My favorite new word is *verge*."

He laughed. "What do you call the side of the road?"

"The shoulder."

"I like that, the shoulder, like on a body."

He looked at his watch. "I fear I must go back to work. But let me ask you one last question. Of all the things you've seen, what has impressed you the most about our country?"

"A thing that has impressed me?"

"Yes, we're working on a new advertising campaign, specifically for the States, and I could use your input. What might we mention about England that would be a draw to intelligent Americans?"

Intelligent Americans. What more does a librarian want to be? I thought about all I had noticed on my trip. "The small shops," I finally said. "That's been my favorite thing."

He reared back. "Small shops?"

"Yes, I have a feeling they're disappearing here too, but you still have so many more than we do at home. Boutiques that focus on selling a few specific items. Stores that only sell old books, pharmacies that are just that, a shop for candles or soaps. Small boutiques that sell women's lingerie. Not a department store that sells everything, and certainly not a mall."

He tapped his finger on his cheek. "I like that. We are not a mall. Although one never wants to use a negative in promotion. Maybe something like, We have what you want, in small bites."

"That sounds good," I assured him.

"So what do you have planned next?" he asked.

"Well, speaking of small shops, I'm going to Hay-on-Wye with some friends."

"Oh, yes, the book place. Never been there, but

heard it's terrific. You should enjoy that. Books galore." He asked one last question: "Going with someone special?"

I thought for a moment, then said, "One can only hope."

TWENTY-SIX

Really Blue Annette

In those few minutes, the earth had turned just that tiny little fraction that made me look at everything differently. I was smelling flowers in the Chelsea Flower Show and a handsome gentleman had talked to me. I was off to Hay-on-Wye to look at books to my heart's content, even if Caldwell was bringing his girlfriend.

I might have set in motion a plot to kill my former boyfriend, which was the only thing standing in my way of utterly enjoying this moment. And I had almost killed myself by smelling a foxglove. Which, of course, made me think of finding out what had happened to Mr. Worth. Being an expert on flowers, he would never have smelled a foxglove—or would he have? Maybe, if he hadn't known that was what he was smelling.

And now it was time to go watch Annette Worth accept the President's Award for her late husband's rose. I followed the sign to the bandstand, and as I looked over the crowd gathered for the award ceremony, I spotted two Brillo Pad grayheads—the Tweedles. Of course they would be there.

When I walked up behind them I saw that Betty was patting Barb's shoulder and Barb was leaking tears. I didn't make my presence known until Barb had calmed down and the tears had been wiped away.

"Hi there," I said.

"Oh," they both turned and looked at me as if they had been caught doing something bad.

"Isn't this exciting?" I asked.

"Yes, but also so unfair," Betty said.

"Howard should have been . . ." And with these words Barb started leaking again.

Betty whispered to me. "She was very fond of him. You might say they had been engaged. There had even been talk of him naming a rose after her—Barely Blue Barb."

I held my breath as I took that name in, then I asked, "What happened to their engagement?"

"Well, first there was Caldwell's Sally, and then Annette. But Barb never gave up hope."

"I did give up hope," Barb said. "I gave it up many times. But then I'd see Howard again and it would come rushing back."

"This must be very hard for you," I said.

Barb nodded.

"She should be standing up there, not that nitwit Annette," Betty spit out between tight teeth. "I wish she'd get rose-thorn disease. That can happen, you know."

Her vehemence surprised me and I didn't know what to say so I turned my attention to the stage. A tall, thin, handsome man was calling us to order. A rather wilted-looking Annette was standing off to the side of the stage. She was wearing a black dress with a dark purple rose pinned to her chest. The rose looked slightly wilted too.

"In honor of this marvelous hybridization of the Almost Blue Annette, I would like to present Howard Worth with the President's Award. As many of you know, Mr. Worth passed away recently and we are so sorry for this loss to his family, his many friends, and of course the world of rose culture. Here to accept the award is his lovely widow, Annette Worth."

Annette came forward and accepted the statue,

which was a gilded rose on a stem. Then the announcer led her to the microphone. I noticed he held her hand and didn't let go as she stood there, looking at the microphone. She stared at it as if it were some kind of flower she couldn't identify. Finally she lifted her head and gazed out at the gathered crowd. My heart went out to her. She did not want to be there and I could tell she was on the verge of tears.

She swallowed and said, "Howard would be so pleased. Roses were his life. Flowers gave him such great joy. I know he will be missed. Thank you."

She stumbled as she stepped down from the podium, but the announcer caught her arm and steadied her. Then, with what seemed like affection, he wrapped a protective arm around her.

Betty sniffed. "Not bad."

I felt compelled to speak in Annette's defense. "Short and sweet. I found it moving."

Barb blurted, "But what about all his hard work. How he managed to do this. She said nothing about what actually went into this accomplishment."

"She didn't know," said Betty.

"She did her best," I murmured.

"It wasn't good enough," Barb barked and started to walk away.

"It should have been Barb up there," Betty said. "She would have known what to say."

"Who was the man who announced her?" I asked.

"Oh him. Lionel Warner-Morehead. Goes by Lion. Pretentious. He's some sort of donor, very important. A follower of Howard's," Barb said.

"And of Annette's," Betty added.

TWENTY-SEVEN

In the Gloaming

After the flower show I decided to go to the Victoria and Albert Museum, where I could have pitched a tent and lived for a few weeks going through the amazing collections of needlework and swords and tiles and other ceramics and costumes and paintings. The list is longer than endless. When the museum closed, I stopped at a cozy street-side café and had a rather greasy meal of fish and chips, then caught the tube back to the B and B.

When I let myself in, the house was so quiet I thought I was alone. I walked back to the sitting room to see how the garden looked in the gloaming and found Caldwell cozily ensconced in his chair with a book in his lap and a bottle of sherry. However, he wasn't reading. He was staring out at the falling dark, but lifted his head and smiled when I entered the room.

"I was hoping you might turn up," he said. "No one else is here yet."

Caldwell wore an old gray sweater, fawn-colored corduroy pants, and worn leather slippers. He looked comfortable and familiar. I thought nothing could be better than talking to him and sharing a glass of sherry. The sight of him there in the fading light made my heart lighter—there were men who knew how to live easily in the world and enjoy it.

Without asking if he should, he poured me some sherry in a delicate, etched glass and handed it over to me.

"How was your day?" he asked.

I didn't want to tell him about being ass-canned in the Holiday Inn. "I just spent a few hours at the Victoria and Albert," I said. "This country is just so old. There are such a lot of accumulated artifacts here. And I'm one who loves all such old things—"

"Old things?"

"All the things we need around us to live, all the objects we cherish and like to look at every day:

books, rugs, shawls, pillows, stools, figurines, toys, bowls. You know, things we hold in our hands and touch and love. Seems to me we live better if we're surrounded by beautiful things."

He nodded, looking right at me. "I love it too. Your so-called stuff."

I took a sip of the sherry and then looked at the glass it was delivered in. "Speaking of good stuff, these are beautiful glasses."

"Passed down in my father's family. I only have two left." He held his out and I carefully touched it with mine. "I believe they are George III."

"And speaking of him—George III, not your father," I said, "I thought of Capability Brown because I went to the Chelsea Flower Show."

"I didn't know you were interested in flowers too. You did hear about our arum lily coming into bloom, didn't you?"

When the first titan arum bloomed in the late 1990s, I had checked online every day to see how the stinking, enormous flower was coming along, entranced both by the size of the flower—the biggest blossom in the world at over three feet tall—and the descriptions of its awful scent. "Yes, how exciting. Did you get a chance to see it? I guess maybe I should say smell it?"

"I did. I stood in a queue for what seemed forever

until finally I was allowed to walk into the greenhouse and smell the foul odor of a thousand rotting pig carcasses. But it was worth it."

"I bet."

"They're hoping for another blossoming this autumn."

"I would love to see that." I took another sip of sherry. Had my taste buds come to life? This sherry tasted better than any I had ever had. "Wow, this is good."

"Glad you like it."

"I saw Barb and Betty at the flower show, and, of course, Annette."

"How was she managing?"

"She's not here, is she?" I didn't want to say anything if she could hear me.

"No, not yet. She had to make some arrangements for the body to be shipped home. I think some friend was helping her and then was going to take her out to dinner, whether she wanted to go or not."

"Lionel?"

"That might have been the one."

"I thought she did fine. Certainly out of her depth, but understandably. But Betty and Barb were not so kind. Did you know there was something going on between Howard Worth and Barb?"

Caldwell sighed. "It was totally one direction. Barb in her own awkward way was very taken with him. He didn't mind talking flowers with her, but that's as far as it went. She suffered through him leaving with Sally and then somehow thought she had got him back when that ended. But when she got the wedding invitation in the States that he was going to marry Annette, I think she finally saw that he wasn't for her."

"She seemed terribly upset today. I don't think she was quite over him." I looked around the room. "Where is Francine?"

"Francine had lots of business meetings today. She said she might be late. That might mean very late."

"She seems nice," I said, while I thought the opposite.

"She can be," he said. "She is a very bright and determined businesswoman. I have learned a lot from her."

Again I didn't want to learn what he had learned from her so I asked, "What does she do?"

"She handles a line of table linens. Very upmarket. They're quite attractive, but the big thing about them is they're covered with a coating of something. Which means that you can spill gravy or wine on them and then wipe it straight off. She's started marketing them here in England and comes over about once every two months to meet with clients. She's also been helping me take a new look at my life."

I wasn't sure how much more I wanted to know about her. "I've been meaning to ask you—what do you do besides running this place? For fun. Not that running a B and B isn't a lot of work; maybe it keeps you completely busy."

Caldwell thought for a second, then waved toward the windows. "Well, there's the garden; I potter away at it rather ineffectively. And then I have my books."

"Yes, you have a terrific selection of books. I've been enjoying the small library in my room."

"I've thought of doing more with them—a bit of buying and selling—but it's hard on one's own. I'm just not sure I'm up to it."

I took another sip of sherry, thinking about being on my own again. For a moment I pictured my life when I went back home, working every day at the library, coming home to an empty house, having to make dinner for one. Dave and I hadn't spent every night together, but three or four nights a week we would do something—go out to eat, grill at his house, I'd make us dinner, go catch a movie. Half my evenings were filled with him and the other half I enjoyed being alone. Now, if Rosie had a boyfriend, she'd be too busy to hang out with me. "I know what you mean. Takes energy to be alone."

The dark was settling in more thoroughly. Caldwell hadn't turned on any lights in the room and I could barely see him, though he wasn't that far away. His voice rose out of his chair. As if reading my mind, he asked, "How many days left now for you on your trip? Only five?"

"Yes, it's going too fast. But I am looking forward to Hay-on-Wye. I didn't think I would be able to get there. The trains don't go there. I had checked into the bus service, but it would have been quite a complicated trip."

"Our train system is not what it used to be. When I was growing up, you could get anywhere on the trains." I heard him sigh and wondered if he was thinking about the trains, but he said, "I've been enjoying your stay."

I flushed and wondered if it was the sherry making me warm. "You have made me feel very welcome here."

"I'm glad." He cleared his throat and added, "I'm sorry that your friend Dave wasn't able to come along with you."

Dave. Funny to hear his name come out of Caldwell's mouth. I was so done with Dave. It was time to come clean. There was no reason not to tell

Caldwell what had actually happened, leaving out the gory details. No need to explain about my inadvertent hit man, if Guy was even that. At least, not yet. "Well, yes, Dave—"

Right then the front door pushed open and the hall light came on. Sharp pointy heels hit the flagstone in the entryway. A wire-thin French voice yahooed, "Caldwell. *Bonsoir.* I'm arrived."

We both sat up straighter in our chairs, as if we'd been caught at something. Francine stood in the doorway to the sitting room. "But it is very dark. You cannot see at all. The light, it does not work?"

Francine switched on the overhead lights and the glare made me blink. She walked into the room like a whirlwind, dressed in a formfitting tweed suit that could have come right off the runway. Her scent permeated everything—sandalwood, with a hint of roses. Francine's presence took over the small space.

Spying the bottle of sherry, she clapped her hands. "*Parfait.* Just what I was wanting. The aperitif. *Cheri,* please to pour me some."

"Get yourself a glass, Francine." Caldwell uncorked the bottle.

She turned and opened a cabinet. With slight distress, I noticed that she knew right where the glasses were.

* * *

After listening to Francine tell us about her day, the meetings, the stores she had gone to with samples of her newest tablecloths, Caldwell stood up and said, "Ladies, I'm off to bed. Please feel free to have more sherry."

"I should go too," I said, not wanting to be left alone with Francine.

She reached out her long fingers and pressed her hand down on top of mine. "Oh, please stay. I don't want to drink all by myself. Plus, we have not really had a chance to talk."

She fascinated me, this elegant Frenchwoman, and I couldn't bring myself to say no. I sank back into my chair. Caldwell stood in the doorway and said good night.

Francine blew him a kiss and said, *"Fait de beaux rêves, rêve de moi."*

The phrase sounded beautiful, especially coming out of her mouth, but I wanted to know what it meant. "Can you translate that for me?"

"Just one of those little things the parents say when the children go to bed, you know. Funny things. It means, Make beautiful dreams, dream of me."

Much more poetic than "Don't let the bed bugs bite," I thought.

Francine poured herself another glassful of sherry. "How are you finding this side of the ocean?"

"In some ways not very different from where I live."

"Really?"

"So many of the same shops, the same clothes. We really are living in such a global economy now."

"I know what you mean. Next I will be selling my linens to everyone in America. The market is enorme."

I didn't correct her English since my French was pretty much nonexistent. I finished off the last little sip of sherry in my glass. My long day was catching up to me. I could feel myself fading away while Francine looked like she could go all night.

"As I have told you, I love the mysteries. May I buy your books here in England?" she asked. "Or perhaps even in France?"

"My books?" I asked before I could stop myself.

"Yes, you are the writer, no?"

"Yes, I write, but I'm not sure if they are here. Not usually published in foreign countries. Not my latest one at least," I scrambled, trying to sound like I knew what I was talking about.

"It is coming out soon?"

"Yes," I said. "Right after I go home."

"I am not so much the reader, but Caldwell likes the books," Francine said. "Maybe too much."

"Yes, I know."

"He is truly a gentle man," she said, giving me a stare.

"I think he is too."

"After this horrible woman left him—he tells you about this Sally woman, yes? He was very, very sad."

"Was he mad at Howard Worth?"

Francine thought for a moment. "I would guess he was mad, but I'm not sure he really blamed Howard. Sally was a restless woman."

"How long have you known him?" I asked, fearing the answer.

"I have been knowing him for a year or so now. We are getting quite close," she said.

She was obviously staking out her territory. I wondered if she felt threatened by me. "Good."

"I'm a very busy woman, but I make the time to come and stay with him."

"He has made a comfortable place here."

"He knows how to do that," she said. "He has always been comforting for me too. Is that how you say it in English?"

I nodded. Francine was certainly clarifying their relationship for me. At least her side of it. I now knew that Francine wanted Caldwell. But I still wasn't sure how he felt about her.

"Well, I'm off to bed." I stood up and knocked over my empty sherry glass. Caldwell's father's glass.

I would have felt terrible if I had broken it, but I caught it in time.

Francine sat like a cat, watching me, and, after another swallow of sherry, said, "Be very careful. You don't want to break anything." She paused, turning her glass around in her hands. "Caldwell, he is like an enfant terrible about breaking his delicacies. The temper he has is *incroyable*."

❧

TWENTY-EIGHT

Analysis of the List

When I crawled into bed and thought of having to spend a whole day with Francine and her catty ways, I almost decided not to go to Hay-on-Wye. I wasn't sure I could stand to watch Francine and Caldwell together all day long. But the lure of all the books I might find won out in the end. I couldn't give up this opportunity, which might be, literally, a once in a lifetime for me.

I plumped up the covers on the bed, got out my notebook, and started to make a list of books I hoped to find.

When I had filled a page with titles, I called Rosie to get a report on her sort-of date. Because of the time difference, I figured I'd catch her on her lunch break at the library. She picked up on the first ring.

"Hey," she said.

"Hey yourself. How's it going?"

"It was a date," she said.

"What makes you so sure now?"

"Because he kissed me."

I pulled myself up in bed. This was good. "Excellent. Do you still like him after spending this time with him?"

"Are you asking me as in—I wouldn't want to join a club that would have me for a member?"

"Well, not really that, but you can be rather skittish," I said, remembering the time she had bolted in the middle of a coffee date, telling me later that he had asked her what she wanted to do with her life and she thought that was too probing.

"Richard has good boundaries."

"So he's standoffish too. Perfect. With you two keeping each other at arm's length, how was the date? Give me the gory."

"You know what's weird is it was rather awful. The movie was super bad, but we started laughing and couldn't stop. Finally we just had to leave. Then we went to Sawatdee and Richard ordered a curry that was so hot, he turned completely red. I swear steam was coming out his ears. He had to go outside for a few minutes to recover. When we got to my house, he was too perfect a gentleman. I had to jump him, but he joined in immediately."

"Did it lead to a stay-over?"

"No, just some heavy petting."

"How old-fashioned. Any future plans?"

"Well, he already asked me out again. He's been texting me all morning. Nancy, priss-butt herself, has been giving me dirty looks, but I don't care. She won't fire me as long as you're gone and she needs me."

"She can't fire you. I'm your boss."

"Oh, yeah. But now I'm worried about you. How are you doing? Did you find Dave?"

I told her about how Honey had thumped me and knocked me over. I also told her about the scene at the Chelsea Flower Show. And I told her about Francine's thinly veiled threat, to watch out not to break anything, and me wondering if it was my body or my spirit that she was worried about breaking.

"Rosie, this is a dangerous place, this England. If you don't watch it, you'll inadvertently kill someone or be killed. I've already tripped over one dead body. And I'm starting to think Howard might have been killed. All the people who were there that night, with the exception of me of course, had a motive for killing him. Plus, he wrote that cryptic note in the book he was reading, as if he knew something. I don't like it."

"Really? You think he might have been killed? Maybe you should move to a different B and B."

"Oh, I think I'm safe enough. And there's Caldwell. . . ."

"Well, I'd say enjoy your vacation while you can. Nancy's been piling work on your desk lately. Now it looks as if you're going to have to work months to make up for the time you've been gone."

"I don't care. I'm going to Hay-on-Wye. With Caldwell and Francine."

"You told me about that town with all the bookstores. Sounds like fun. If you see something I might like, get it for me, would you please? I'd love an old book from England."

"Absolutely. I'll add it to my already quite long list. In return, why don't you walk by my desk and accidentally knock all the work on the floor?"

"Oh, she'd make me pick it up. Try not to kill or get killed on your trip to book land."

After my first cup of tea in the morning, I casually opened the back door to the garden and strolled down the path. I was quite sure I had seen the foxglove flowers when I looked out the window, but I had never been out in the garden to check. A veritable cottage garden had been created, a mixture of all the bright and glorious flowers that bloomed in England. But it did look a little overgrown. Caldwell said he didn't do enough with it.

Toward the back, standing upright as soldiers, was a patch of foxglove, at nearly five feet tall, hard to miss. The purple blooms looked like the finger pads we librarians wore to get through a sheaf of papers fast. I walked as close as I could get to them on the path, then eased my way through the flowers to stand right by them, making sure to hold my breath.

Toward the top of the plant, right under the blooms, it looked like leaves had been taken off of a couple of the plants. Could have been bugs, could have been wind, but I was guessing it was hands that had gathered the toxic leaves. What was I to do about it? Who could I tell? The coroner had declared Howard Worth's death the result of an accidental overdose; why would I suggest otherwise?

I heard Caldwell calling me from the front of the house, so I scurried out of the flowers, quickly slipped through the door, and went back to the sitting room. It was eight o'clock sharp, just when he'd said we would depart.

I went out front and found that Caldwell had pulled his car up to the front of the house. I climbed into the front seat. Caldwell had warned me that we would probably encounter rain, so I'd dressed for it. I had on my Burberry raincoat and my lime-green walking shoes, which were also waterproof. I'd come to think of them as frog shoes.

Not knowing what to do with my hair in this weather, I had pulled it back in a couple barrettes, which oddly made me look younger than usual, like a schoolgirl. Since my coat had a hood, I wouldn't be needing a hat.

Caldwell gave me the once-over, then nodded. "Very appropriate. You look like you're ready to go hunting."

I thought of the hunt I had just done and of the discovery I had made, but pushed it out of my mind. I would think of it all later. Today I would enjoy myself. "Maybe we should call it 'booking.'"

He laughed harder than my very small joke demanded, but in such a pleasant way that I didn't think less of him for it. I could tell he, like myself, was all keyed up about this trip.

Caldwell looked every inch the English countryman. He was wearing one of those amazing waxed cotton coats that makes a great crackling noise when you move in them, like the sound of a million blackbird wings.

I so didn't want to think that he had anything to do with Howard's death, but I had to ask a few questions. "Your garden is so lovely right now," I said.

"Thanks. I wish I could take more of the credit. I have a bloke who comes and fusses with it every few weeks. It doesn't look as good as it used to when Sally—" He broke off.

"Is that foxglove I see toward the back?" I asked.

"Might be. I haven't a clue. Ask Barb or Betty. They're sure to know."

His nonchalance about my questions would seem hard to manage unless one were a very good actor. Caldwell was good at so many things, but I doubted that.

He had brought a thermos of tea and he poured us each a cup. I wasn't sure why we weren't having our tea inside, but then I just figured it was part of the adventure. As we sipped, we waited for Francine.

Finally I had to ask, "Why are we sitting out here? I mean, it's quite pleasant, but will Francine know we're out here?" I was enjoying the intimacy of the small car, the shared tea.

"She doesn't like to get up in the morning," he explained. "She's less apt to dilly-dally if she's knows we're waiting for her in the car. I shouted this information through her door. I did hear her moving around in her room, which was a good sign. Also, I told her we were leaving in ten minutes with or without her."

"We wouldn't leave without her, would we?"

"We won't have to. Francine is very good with deadlines."

"I had trouble getting to sleep last night, so I sat up in bed and made a shopping list," I said.

"Oh, may I see it?" He reached into one of the many pockets on his coat and pulled out a long list of his own.

We exchanged lists. I was happy to see there weren't too many duplicates, so we wouldn't be in serious competition with each other. As I checked over his list, I was happy to see that nearly half of the authors on it were women, many Americans too: Marilyn Robinson, Jane Smiley, Ruth Hamilton, Louise Erdrich. Not just American, but Midwesterners. I wondered if his selection had been compiled for my benefit. If so, it was a sweet gesture and appreciated.

Caldwell was murmuring over my list. Finally he looked up. "Good," he said. "Yes, very nice indeed."

"You approve?" I asked, laughing.

"Not that you need my approval, but it's an interesting list, revealing of your character."

"Oh, I see. Some people read palms, others analyze Rorschach blots, you are able to know an individual by what books they buy?"

"Something like that," he said, a little embarrassed.

"So what do you now know about me?"

"You have good taste, evidenced by the Harding. A vast spectrum of interest, ranging from the noir books of Highsmith to poems of Wordsworth. You know your books. John Cowper Powys is pretty esoteric, and you like to have fun—Barbara Pym. You are kind, but with a slight edge, that comes through with the Gerald Durrell, and his brother Lawrence. Also a little old-fashioned, as there are not many contemporary writers on your list."

"That's amazing. You see all that in my list?"

"Well, I must admit it takes some extrapolating." He slapped the list in his hand. "But the odd thing is that these are all British writers."

"When in Britain . . . ," I started, knowing I didn't need to finish.

When he handed my list back, our hands brushed, and I felt a small jolt. He looked up suddenly and his eyes opened wider, really taking me in. I wondered if he had felt the electricity too. I would miss him when I went home.

Before either of us could say anything, I heard a tapping on my car window. Francine stood in the street, not looking her best. Her makeup was blurry and her hair seemed cattywampus. She was dressed in some sort of poncho over a tight skirt with high-heeled boots. I wondered where she thought she was going. Then I wondered how much of the sherry had remained in the bottle last night.

"I must sit there." She opened my door and pointed at my seat. "Otherwise, I will have a terrible badness in my head from the movement of the car. It would not be pleasant for anyone."

She stepped back as I climbed out of the car and lifted up the seat to crawl into the back. Even though I wasn't that big, I felt like I was cramming into the small backseat. It was so tight that I wasn't sure two people could even fit. Caldwell had stuffed several book bags with various shop names on them in the back, I assumed for us to carry our haul home in.

The sky was overcast and as we left the city, it started to rain, a gentle patter. I found it soothing, but Francine was fussing.

"Zut, my coiffure," she said, patting at her hair.

I found myself staring at the back of Caldwell's head, noticing how nicely shaped it was. When I leaned forward to hear their conversation, I would get a whiff of his smell—a hint of smokiness, a delicate scent of the binding of old books, and some gentle sweetness like early violets.

What was happening to me, I wondered. Was I noticing what a fine man Caldwell was because Francine had laid claim to him? Or was it because I had really let go of Dave? Or was it possibly because Andrew had noticed me yesterday and I realized that I deserved to have a nice man in my life?

I leaned back into my small nest of a seat and watched Francine talk. Her hands flew about the car like a flock of sparrows and her voice, while I couldn't catch all the words, sounded like a squeaky wheel, slightly raspy but not completely unpleasant. I could see why Caldwell liked her. She brought so much energy and life with her even when she wasn't at her best. I stood no chance against such an elegant, vivacious woman and I tried to feel happy for Caldwell, but it was hard.

TWENTY-NINE

The Right Book

My first glimpse of Hay-on-Wye was over the Wye River, the town covered in a misty rain, and the old ruins of Hay castle standing stout in the gloom, solid and stony. The atmosphere was muted and brooding—it could not have been a more perfect day to poke around in bookstores.

Caldwell parked by a pub called the Old Black Lion, pointed at it, and said we should all meet there for lunch in two hours. I already knew the bookstore I wanted to start at—the Sensible Book-shop. The name alone was intriguing. I was very clear that I did not want to be a tagalong with Francine and Caldwell. Talk about being a third wheel.

I stepped out of the car, didn't wait for them to make any suggestions about where to go. I had my bearings from a map I had printed out from the Internet and tucked into one of my guidebooks. I waved good-bye and left them.

When I was a block away, I saw that Francine had still only put one foot out of the car and that Caldwell was leaning over, talking to her, and holding her hand as if ready to help her out of the car. I had seen enough. In two hours I could get some serious shopping done.

With only a half an hour to go until lunch, I was sitting on the floor of the third bookstore I had gone into, this one specializing in older scientific books. I was looking for a book on flowers for Rosie, preferably with nice illustrations of roses. Her birthday was coming up.

I glanced over a couple of rows and a book title caught my eye: *A Manual of Technical Plumbing and Sanitary Science*. Dave would have loved that. It had been my habit to buy old plumbing books for him and he had quite a library. When I had first met him, he'd had only a few paperback books in his house. But it was like I always said to Rosie: You can make anyone a reader if you match them up with the right book.

But as I sat and pondered that statement, I saw it might also be true with people—that the match had to be right.

I had tried to make Dave into a man I could love. We had both tried to find ways of being together, of connecting with each other, but we had ultimately been very different. He liked to watch sports and drink a good brew; I preferred listening to classical music, sipping a rich merlot, and reading.

I actually saw reading as a shared activity, having grown up with a best friend who would read next to me on her family's couch while we ate cinnamon toast and drank hot chocolate. My whole family read together in our living room, flopped in various positions on chairs, couches, and floors. I thought everyone read together.

But Dave saw my reading as a defense against him. He hated it when I read in bed. How had I thought I could marry such a man?

A sadness at the time we had both wasted swept over me and I started to cry. Not a fierce sobbing, but, more like the constant rain outside, a gentle, nurturing cry that ended with a few sniffles and a good nose-blowing, leaving me feeling cleansed and oddly hopeful.

I looked around and realized I was right where I wanted to be—sitting on the floor of a cold and grubby bookstore in Wales, looking at the tattered covers of old books while it rained outside. Even though I was alone, I was happy. I was in a world I knew and loved, the world of books.

Turning back to the shelf that held botanical books, I found a turn-of-the-last-century book with delicate line drawings of roses and other flowers. As I paged through it I noticed that some of the roses had been colored in with notations on the side of those pages, a date, a place. A previous owner had recorded her life with roses. I knew I had found the right book for Rosie.

I turned to the listing on foxgloves, *Digitalis purpurea;* otherwise known as Lion's Mouth, Fairy Fingers, and then I saw, *Deadman's Bells.* Not Balls.

I stifled a gasp as the significance of Howard's message sank in, then read on: "The leaves have a slight characteristic odor and a strong nauseous bitter taste. Only the second year's growth of leaves are used medicinally. They yield the well-known drug digitalin. . . . These leaves, however, are very powerful and poisonous and should only be employed by skilled physicians. They are too dangerous for domestic use or self-medication."

I bent my head over the book and pondered. What did it all mean? What was I to do? Why had Howard written those words in *Winnie-the-Pooh?* Had he known what was happening to him?

I had a slight flush of sadness as I thought about Howard. Poor man. What could I do for him now?

"I think I figured something out."

"I hope you're talking about Dave," Rosie said.

"That too. But listen, I found out that foxglove is called Deadman's Bells."

"Oh, that is fascinating," Rosie said, then waited for me to explain.

I was sitting on the floor, leaning against a shelf of books, tucked in the back of a bookstore where I hoped no one could hear me talking on my cell phone. I slowly went through it all: finding Howard, Winnie-the-Pooh, Deadman's Balls, deadly foxglove, digitalis, and realizing I had misread what Howard had written—his last words, possibly.

I cleared my throat. "Now I just have to figure out what to do next."

"You sound funny. Have you been crying?"

"Why do you ask?"

"I can hear it in your voice."

"Just a trickle. Nothing serious. A feeling sorry for Howard and, I guess, myself kind of cry. What am I going to do?"

"Tell someone."

"Oh, God, Rosie, but I don't trust anyone. They all have reason to want Howard dead. Except Francine, and I don't have a good relationship with her."

"Even Caldwell?"

"Unfortunately yes. Howard stole his girlfriend away from him years ago."

"That's a long time."

"Sometimes feelings can last a long time."

"I guess you're right," she said, then fell quiet.

"What?" I asked.

"Well, I have the opposite problem. I'm trying to figure out how not to bolt from Richard." She took a deep breath, then burst out with, "I really like this guy and that scares me and when I get scared I don't like to stick around and so I find some reason to not like him and I don't want to do that."

"At least you don't think he might have killed someone."

"So you *like* like Caldwell."

"Um . . . maybe."

"Well, then you better clear his name. Find out who killed Howard, if you really think that's what happened. And deal with that French femme."

"And you hang in with Richard."

"Deal."

When I walked into the pub where we had planned on meeting, only Francine was waiting there. She waved me over.

"I could not stand it," she said. An empty plate sat in front of her with a half-finished cup of coffee. "I do not like these shops filled with books I do not want to read. Besides, being dark and dirty, they are very smelly, like unwashed clothes. I was hungry and so I came here and ate some sort of fried fishes."

I sat down, tucking my bag of books under the table. I thought of arguing with her about the smell in the bookstores—which I found much more like a favorite old sweater—but maybe we were describing the same fragrance.

"I understand," I said though I didn't at all. "Where is Caldwell? Have you seen him?"

"I left him back there in the bowels of a store. He was being devoured by the books. That man," she said, shaking her head. "He doesn't really seem to live in the real world."

I nodded, but I was getting a little angry with her. Here she was with the nicest man in the world and she was complaining about him.

"I'm going back to London," she announced.

"How?"

"There is a bus leaving. The man at the bar told me. Please tell Caldwell that I have departed." Francine stood up and gathered her belongings.

She couldn't desert Caldwell like that, without saying anything. My voice rose in spite of myself. I came close to screaming at her in a very loud whisper. "Aren't you going to wait and tell him yourself? How can you treat him like that, when he cares about you? Deserting him without telling him why."

She stared at me. "What are you talking about?"

"I think it's horrible of you to leave him here. All alone. How do you think he will feel?"

"But you will be here. He's not alone. He will feel fine."

I could see that she was choosing not to understand me. "Yes, but it's not the same. After all, you two are like a couple. He's counting on you."

She shook her head. "We're not a couple."

"You're not?"

"But of course not. At one time I thought maybe it could be, but then I saw we are not meant for each other. It would be very bad if we tried to be together. I have too much of the energy and he is too calm. We pull in very different directions."

"Oh," I said and sat down. "Being pulled in different directions. I know what you mean."

"Caldwell is very good to me. We have helped each other out from time to time, but that is all."

"Before you leave can I ask you a question?"

"Certainly," she said.

"Do you think Caldwell could kill someone?"

"But of course!"

"You do?" I wondered what she knew.

"Silly question." She shook her head. "Everyone could kill someone. It's just the way we're made."

"Would he have killed Howard Worth?"

"Certainly not. Why would he kill that old man? Not any reason."

Suddenly, I believed her, and relief flowed through me like a strong river. How could I ever have thought Caldwell capable of such a thing?

Francine went on. "He liked Howard. In the end he was even glad Sally went away, although it took a while. But now I must go."

"I'm sorry that you didn't enjoy yourself," I said and found I really meant it.

She shrugged. "No, it's nothing. This town is for you and him. Not for me. That much is very clear. Do you see it?"

I wasn't sure what she was talking about, but took a guess. "Yes, we both like books."

"It is not so much about the books." She pulled on her coat. "I see more. You have a good mind. Employ it."

I watched her walk out of the pub, swaying on her high heels, pulling her poncho up around her neck. Then she was gone.

I sat still and pondered her words. What had she seen? What was she talking about?

Caldwell walked in a few minutes later, his cheeks rosy and his smile large. He was carrying a very full bag of books. "You must see what I've found."

"I have a few books to show you too."

"Isn't this brilliant?" he asked, sitting down next to me.

I was very happy to see him. "Yes, totally and completely brilliant. Way better than I had imagined."

"I'm starving. Work up quite an appetite shopping. I'd like something warm inside me."

"Me too." I noticed he hadn't asked about Francine. "Oh, Francine decided to catch a bus back to London."

He nodded. "I'm not surprised. I'm not sure why she insisted on coming in the first place. She wouldn't listen to me. But sometimes she has to find out for herself. She's usually a pretty good sport. Did she seem upset?"

"Not particularly. A little cranky."

"Yes, that sounds like Francine. She can turn into a monster if she doesn't get her way." He frowned, then gave me a concerned look. "How about you? Are you ready to leave?"

"Not by a long shot. I could happily spend a week here with you, looking for the right book."

"Yes, I know what you mean," he said, looking at me. "That would be heaven."

THIRTY

Secrets Revealed

We grabbed something to eat and then the rest of that long, luxurious afternoon, Caldwell and I were never more than a bookshelf apart.

He would show me a book, I would nod. I would show him a book, he would shake his head or gleefully take it out of my hands to give it a going-over. Occasionally we would have a short discussion over the pros and cons of a certain book: its age, its condition, its edition. There was never a sense of being bothersome, and always the feeling the other person was available.

I had forgotten how completely comfortable one could be with another person, especially with a man. I wasn't sure I had ever experienced this level of camaraderie before. In short, Caldwell and I were kindred souls.

I felt a small glow of hope that all could be well in the world. But I also had the tugging sense, as if I was being pulled into a dark current, of what I hadn't told Caldwell: that I was really a librarian, that Dave had broken up with me, that I had thought of killing him. And then, worst of all, that I had thought it possible he had killed Howard Worth.

If we were to have any kind of real relationship, I had to tell him these facts about myself.

Finally the shop owner in the Book Nook started to make noises that he was closing.

"They shut early here," Caldwell whispered. "Five-thirty. Must get tea on the table."

"I can't believe it but I'm starving again."

"Well, we've been on our feet all day long. This book hunting is hard work. I'd say we deserve a good meal. What do you fancy?"

"I could eat a horse," I said.

"Since this isn't France, I don't think that will be available. How about fish? Might that do?"

"Yes, please."

"I know the very place. It's a little early, but I'm sure they're open."

We walked to the car, laden with our bags, and stashed our books in the backseat. It was a good thing that Francine had decided to take the bus back to London as I wasn't sure there would have been room for her. There was hardly room for a toy poodle.

We walked over to the Three Tuns, a pub and restaurant dating back to the sixteenth century, Caldwell told me. The whitewashed walls and the dark beams had the look of old England about them.

When we were asked where we would like to sit, I spied the Inglenook chimney and saw that there were seats available by it.

"Oh, let's sit by the fire," I suggested. I was feeling not only hungry, but cold and tired. Caldwell gave me the seat closest to the fire. I could feel the heat on my back like a massaging hand.

I leaned back with a sigh. "Thank you."

"For what?" he asked.

"For this," I waved my arm at the room. "For this whole day. For giving me this seat," I started, then continued, "For taking me to Hay-on-Wye, for being the perfect host, for helping me find some books . . ."

"Whoa," he said. "Go no further. This was no obligation on my part. Quite the opposite. This was all a scheme to get you alone and defenseless in the wilds of Wales, and ask you all the questions about being a writer that I've been wanting to ask during the whole of your stay."

"What?" I said, getting a little worried. I had much to answer for. I picked up the menu and held it in front of my face. "What do you think you're going to have?" I asked. "Oh, look, they have black pudding."

"It's quite nice, that," Caldwell said. "But do you mean you're not going to try the steamed beef and oxtail pudding? Where is your sense of adventure? That might rival your pork pie of the other day."

"Stodgy, you think?"

"I'm sure of it. But made for a day like today."

"I think I will have the fish."

"Sounds good."

The waitress came and took our orders. I ordered the sole and Caldwell followed suit. I asked Caldwell to select a beer for me, trusting his judgment, but to make it just a half-pint.

When the waitress came back with our beers, we clinked them together, said, "Cheers," and then each of us took a healthy swallow. Without waiting for a breath, I dove in, "I have to tell you about me being a writer."

"Good, go on then."

"Well, the fact of the matter is . . ." I had to do this. I took a deep breath, looked him square in the face, noticed his warm eyes, and said, "I'm not."

"Not what?"

"A writer."

"Oh," his brows lifted up on his forehead as he took my statement in.

I held my breath. Why had I told him the truth? I watched as his lips twitched up in an almost smile.

"That's a relief," he said.

"It is? I'm sorry I lied. I don't know why I did. I didn't mean to. I didn't want to fool you or anything. It just came out. I'm on vacation and I didn't want to be myself anymore. Why is it a relief?"

"So what are you?"

My occupation, of which I was proud, seemed hard to say. Revealing who I truly was would bring all that old part of my life back and I would have to face it again. "I'm a librarian."

Caldwell stared at me. "Really, truly?"

"Yup."

The smile broke in full force across his face. "That's fantastic. Much better than a writer."

"Really?"

"Well, if you were a writer, I could only be a fan, but this way—how can I put it?—well, we're more like equals."

"Caldwell, what can you mean by that?"

He screwed up his face. "That didn't come out right. I meant that if you were a writer, you would be in a different league, I might not feel as comfortable with you, that sort of thing. But you're a librarian and that I understand. I thought of being one myself." He beamed at me.

"Really?"

"Yes, it seems like such a noble occupation. I would imagine that you're a killer librarian."

"I try to be."

"Actually, I have a secret that I've been wanting to talk to someone about, someone who might understand what I want to do." He said it so dead seriously that I got worried. What possible secret could he have?

"What?"

"I'm thinking of giving up the B and B."

"Why?"

"Because I'm running out of room."

"How so?"

"Well, the books are taking over. You know that other room on the second floor. I can't rent it out anymore because it's completely filled with books. I mean piled high, in some places to the ceiling. And soon I'm going to have to take over another bedroom to manage my stock. It would be hard to run a B and B with so few rooms to rent. Hardly worth it."

"Stock?"

"Well, that's the other thing. I sell books online. But what I really want to do is open a shop."

"A bookstore?"

"A bookshop."

"How exciting."

The waitress brought our two plates of food. The sole looked pale and delicate on my plate. I was happy to see a large mound of mashed potatoes next to it.

"Does Dave like to shop for books too?" he asked, picking up his fork.

"Dave who?" I asked, then snapped to attention. "Oh, yes, Dave."

"The plumber."

"Well, that's another thing that I haven't been completely truthful about." I took a deep breath. I had to say it. "Dave dumped me."

"Dumped you? What does that mean?"

"Broke up with me. Gave me the boot. Told me to get lost."

"I did understand the phrase. I'm just surprised." Caldwell put down his fork. "I'm sorry. I didn't mean to intrude on your personal life."

"No, I can talk about it now. But when we first

met I was so upset about it I didn't think I could manage to say what had actually happened without bursting into tears, and you didn't really know me and I was trying to hold it together. So I pretended that he just couldn't come. You see, I was all packed and ready for him to pick me up for the airport when he told me he didn't want to be with me anymore."

"What a cur!"

His reaction cheered me up immensely. "Yes, I guess he was."

"I know how you feel. When Sal left me I didn't go out of the house for a month. Didn't want to see anyone, didn't want to have to talk about it at all. The only good thing about that period in my life was that it gave me time to really get my books organized."

"I know what you mean. There's nothing like cataloguing books for taking your mind off of things."

"Exactly. When you said you wanted to kill someone, you weren't doing research for a book?"

"No. There were some moments when I thought I wanted to kill Dave."

"Of course you did. After what he had done to you. It will take you months and months to get over it."

"I'm not sure it will take that long. This trip has helped a great deal. Really given me a new perspective on everything."

"Like what?"

"Well, looking back on my relationship with Dave, I see how it was really a compromise for me. Probably for both of us."

"How's that?"

"I know this will be hard for you to believe, but he didn't like books."

Caldwell shook his head sadly. "It's a shock to realize that there are people like that in the world, isn't it?"

"I don't know how I thought we would be able to really make a go of it—stay together when he didn't even like to see me reading a book. How did Sally feel about your books?"

"I think she was jealous of them. For some reason, she seemed to feel that when I was reading, I was ignoring her."

"Dave was the same way. I don't understand that at all. Reading next to someone can be the most companionable thing to do in all the world."

Caldwell cleared his voice, then launched, "I completely understand about the wanting to kill him part. When Sal left me in the lurch—and I do mean in the lurch, four guests on the way, no food in the house, and not much money left in our joint account—I wanted to do something that would accurately express my feelings at that time. Since she had disappeared I couldn't take it out on her. There was little thinking in what I did next." He paused.

"What?"

"Under cover of night, I took our mattress that we had spent a pretty penny on and had had for less than a year, and tied it to the top of my car. I drove it to the Thames and threw it in."

"You didn't?" I asked.

"Watching that big white barge float away was one of the most gleeful moments in my life. It didn't last more than a second, but I'll never forget it. Occasionally acting out your feelings can be very helpful."

"Very inspiring," I said. My first thought was that he might understand how I talked to Guy about Dave, maybe starting something I didn't intend.

My second thought was that I wanted to kiss him.

∽

THIRTY-ONE

High Praise

A toilet could be a work of art, I reflected as I entered the bathroom stall. I owed this trip to England all to a toilet—the Flush Budget. Hard to believe. A song bubbled inside of me even though I couldn't carry a tune. I had told Caldwell about my real life and warmth had not fled his eyes. In fact, I'd say if anything they shone more brightly at me.

As I washed my hands, the water ran like silk over my fingers. All was well with the world. I hadn't looked at a clock all afternoon. Timeless. I didn't want the day to end.

I took my cell phone out of my pocket and for a moment thought of calling Rosie. The impulse to tell someone what was happening was strong, but I could simply savor it all myself. I'd call her tomorrow.

When I walked back to our table, I saw that a concoction of chocolate in the shape of a castle had been placed between us with two forks.

"I went ahead and ordered," Caldwell said with a pleased smile.

"Perfect," I said.

"It's dark chocolate," he said.

"I thought it might be."

We took a bite together. The richness of the chocolate made me yearn for everything good and tasty in life.

But there was one more thing that needed to be cleared up.

"I've been wondering about Howard," I started.

"Yes, I have been too," he chimed in.

"Do you think it's possible someone killed him?"

"I've been wondering about that. Much as I want his death to be an accident, I just have a feeling about it, that someone is behind it."

"Like what?" I asked, curious what he had gleaned.

"Well, that Annette seems to be getting rather a lot of comforting from a certain handsome man, that

Howard Worth was worth a lot of money, and that the means to getting digitalis were certainly in her hands, literally. And who would know if it was an accident or not?"

"Yes, I agree with all that, but then why would she insist that he couldn't have overdosed, why would she tell everyone that she was in charge of his medications? Seems odd to me to make such a point of that."

"But that could be just to lead them off the trail."

"But no one, except you and me, even thinks he might have been killed. Oh, and the killer." I hesitated but I knew I had to tell him this one last thing. "I even suspected you for a moment."

"Good on you. You are leaving no stone unturned. But I have no access to digitalis."

"But you do," I said.

His face went blank, then turned puzzled. "I do?"

"The foxglove in the garden."

"Which one is that?"

Either he was a master actor or he really didn't know his flowers. "The tall flower with purple blossoms that point downward and look like fingers."

"Toward the back of the garden?"

"Yes."

"It was Sally's garden. I don't have a clue about flowers. But why would it matter if I have foxglove?"

"That's what digitalis comes from."

"Oh, I see."

"Then there's Betty and Barb," I pointed out. "The Tweedles do know their flowers."

"Yes, they're rather keen."

"And Barb was in love with Howard."

"But just in a schoolgirl way."

"Schoolgirls love very seriously."

"You can't really think—" he started.

"I walked back to look at your foxglove and there are leaves missing from the top of the plant. I've looked into it. It doesn't take much to overdose on the drug. It's a very dangerous plant. Why someone told me even a strong inhale of a leaf can kill you."

"My. I had no idea. Why would anyone even put such a flower in a garden? What should we do?" he asked.

"Eat this scrumptious dessert, talk of other things, and when we get back home, ask Betty and Barb some questions."

"Brilliant," he said and took another bite.

We ate it slowly and talked, strolling back through our lives as if we needed to catch up on everything that had brought us to this moment. Caldwell told me about his pet ferret named Dandy, I told him about my grandmother Butty and her peanut butter cookies. He talked about starring in a play at his public school; I bragged about being the editor of my high school newspaper. He described swimming in the sea by Brighton; I tried to tell him how cold it could get in Minnesota in winter.

"Is it so cold that sometimes you don't take off your coat and put it in the boot when you get in the car?" he asked.

"It's so cold that sometimes you don't take your coat off when you get into bed," I told him.

"How high does the snow get?" he asked.

I stood up and reached my hand over my head. "The drifts can reach up to the rooftops."

"This I must see."

I could not bring myself to say anything, afraid I was reading too much into his comment. The thought of Caldwell continuing to be in my life was completely too good to be true.

Finally, at a sign from Caldwell, the waitress slid our bill onto the table. The restaurant was closing around us, most of the tables empty. We were the only ones left sitting by the fire. I didn't want to leave. Never in my life had I been with a man with whom I had so much in common, with whom I did not need to explain the important things in life: books, reading, and chocolate.

"I guess it's time," I said.

"Yes, I think we have to go back." Caldwell pulled

my chair out. "Whether they killed Howard or not, the Tweedles told me they approve of you. You have their blessings."

"What does that mean?" I asked.

"They said that you were a solid, reliable Midwestern woman who had her feet on the ground."

"As dull as a doorknob," I laughed.

"Not at all. Most importantly, they assured me that you were a good person—one to be trusted."

"High praise indeed." I could see them saying it together. "It's obvious they adore you."

"That's because I make them porridge." He shook his head. "I hope they didn't do anything to Howard."

"Let's hope we're both wrong and that it was some sort of accident. Maybe his heart just gave out all on its own."

We stepped out into the night. Rain fell in a spray as fine as mist. I tipped my head back to take it full on my face. Was this all I ever wanted—rain in a town that loved books with a man who understood?

A hand slid into mine and squeezed.

Maybe I wanted more. I squeezed back.

"Let's go home," Caldwell said.

THIRTY-TWO

∞

Hot Toddies

After talking nonstop for most of the ride home, we both fell silent as we drove into London. The rain had stopped and the streets were quiet. I admired Caldwell's confidence as he maneuvered through roundabouts, drove easily on the left side of the road, and always found the appropriate lane for a turn. By this point in the day, I was admiring everything about him.

The silence was cozy.

"What's still on your list?" he asked.

"Do you mean my book list or my things to do in London list?"

"The latter."

"I haven't been to Buckingham Palace."

"Not yet seen the queen?"

"No." I fell silent again.

"Only four days left," he said.

"I know."

"Maybe this weekend we could drive down to Canterbury."

"Where the archbishop is and the cathedral? So much history. I would love to see all that."

"I know where to get the best fish and chips there."

"Any good bookshops?" I asked.

He nodded. I could see his face in the faint light of the dashboard. I wanted to memorize it.

"The Tweedles are leaving tomorrow," he said. "We'll clear everything up with them. I'm sure they did nothing to Howard."

"Oh," I said. "But this will mean no more porridge?"

"Not unless you've developed a yen."

"I'll stick with toast and your good marmalade."

"I don't suppose you could stay any longer," he asked quickly.

I thought for a moment of work, my ticket, the mail piling up, my obligations. "Oh, I wish."

"Just a thought."

I could tell we were getting close to his house. We were off the larger streets and he was making more turns.

"It was hard for me to get away this long," I explained.

"I suppose they need you at the library."

"Unfortunately, they do. The fall ordering has to be done."

He pulled into a small parking space right in front of his house and turned off the car. We both sat still. My hand reached out for his. "I could try."

"Really?" He turned toward me. The stick shift stuck up between us. He touched my face. I leaned toward him.

"Karen?" he whispered.

Our faces bumped and our lips touched for a brief instant.

The door to the B and B swung open and the Tweedles were standing there, waving at us.

As we got out of the car we could hear them saying, "We were waiting for you to get home. Annette's run off with that young man. We knew there was something fishy going on."

Reluctantly we left our stashes of books well secured in the backseat and went into the house.

"What has happened?" Caldwell asked.

The two women jostled in front of him to tell the story.

"She took a bag with her."

"He helped her carry her stuff."

"She wouldn't talk to us, tell us anything."

"He held her hand."

Caldwell looked at them both. "So you don't know where she's gone or even if she's done anything but gone out for dinner?"

"We think more than that. We've been suspecting for some time that she has taken a liking to that guy. Haven't we, Betty?"

Betty just nodded. It was as if she had wound down.

Caldwell went to work in the kitchen, getting us all something to drink. He and I had tea; the Tweedles went for hot toddies. They had brought their own stash of bourbon. They insisted that Caldwell try the bourbon and he took a swig, then wrinkled his nose. "Nasty stuff."

"Howard liked it if it was made into a hot toddy."

We all adjourned to the back room. After a sip of our drinks, I decided it was time to ask the Tweedles some questions. I'd start out easy. "Did you make a hot toddy for Howard that last night?"

Betty nodded. "Yes, he said he was going to have trouble sleeping. I wanted to make sure he didn't."

"But I made him one," said Barb.

"You too?"

"Yes, you had gone to sleep."

"Two hot toddies?" Caldwell joined in.

Before I started to lose track of who was talking I asked, "What did you put in the hot toddies? Any extraspecial ingredient?"

They both turned and looked at me.

I decided the best way to handle this was to put it to them straight. Neither of them seemed like the type to be able to lie. So I asked, "Barb, did you put any foxglove in his drink?"

"No, I did," Betty said. "I put just a titch of fox-glove in his drink. Just enough to make him sick."

"But I did too," Barb jumped in.

"From Caldwell's garden?" I asked.

They both nodded.

"Why?" I asked.

The Tweedles looked at each other. It was as if Caldwell and I weren't in the room.

"Because he hurt you," Betty said. "Why did you do it?"

"Because I wanted to teach him a lesson. I was still mad about him marrying Annette. Give him a taste of his own medicine."

"I didn't mean to kill him."

"I didn't think he'd die. I just wanted to give him

a bit of a fright. Make him think twice about what he had done to me."

"It wasn't very much. Just a pinch."

"I was so careful to put only a dash in the drink."

"He didn't seem to notice it."

"He drank it right down."

"I did it for you."

"I did it for us. So he would know what it felt like to be hurt."

They threw their arms around each other and started to cry.

Caldwell and I looked at each other. He made a face and took a sip of his tea. I followed suit.

Finally, deflated, the two Tweedles sank down into chairs. "What's going to happen now?"

"Well, we have to tell someone," Caldwell said.

"I suppose," Betty agreed.

"It's the right thing to do," Barb added.

"You didn't mean to kill him?" I asked, feeling sorry for them in their predicament, understanding it a little too much for my comfort.

"Oh, no, not Howard."

"We really both loved him, in our own ways."

When we were done with our drinks, Caldwell called the police.

THIRTY-THREE

Kidnapped

I'd be surprised if the Tweedles got much time at all," Caldwell said the next night as we sat at what we now considered our curry place, the restaurant we had gone to eat at my first night in London. We had just finished our meal. I was pretty sure we were on a date.

"Hopefully, they'll be able to share a cell," I said.

"Yes, it would be awful to think of them as being apart."

"The police were very gentle with them last night," I said.

"We'll know more in a few days. I hope they settle out of court. I don't want to have to say anything against them, poor old dears."

"I agree with you, but they are experts on flowers, and they must have had a sense of the danger they were putting him in."

"They loved roses. I'm not sure they knew a whole lot about foxglove. But that's for the court to find out."

I had excused myself to go to the loo halfway through dinner and by this devious means had already paid for the meal.

"We just need the check," he said.

"I've taken care of it," I proudly announced.

"Why, you little cheeky thing, you. How did you manage?"

"I have my ways."

"Feel like going to the pub?" he asked.

"Oh, I don't know. A hot toddy in front of the fire sounds good."

"How about a glass of wine?"

"Even better."

We had only just settled, sitting very close together on the love seat in front of the fire, when a blare of the William Tell overture jolted out of my pocket. We jumped apart. It took me a second to recognize my cell phone ring.

"It's my phone," I said. "It never rings."

"You'd better answer it."

"Let me just see who it is," I pulled out the cell phone. The number I saw was all too familiar. "It's Dave."

"Blast him," Caldwell said.

"I'll get rid of him." I had to answer it. After all, he might be in trouble because of me.

"Yes?" I said.

Dave's voice came booming over the line, loud music playing in the background. "Karen, Kirstin's gone missing. That guy took her."

"What guy?"

"The one you warned me about, the guy with blond hair. He's taken Kirstin. I saw him talk to her and the next minute she was gone."

"Where are you?"

"At a pub across the street from the hotel. I don't know what to do."

I looked at Caldwell and he was watching me carefully. "How long has she been gone?"

"It just happened. You have to help me. This is all your fault. What if he hurts her?"

"Why would he take her?"

Dave's voice cracked. "How would I know? What did you tell him? How could you do this to me?"

He was right. It was all my fault. Somehow my

conversation with Guy had activated something in him that was ending up with a missing woman. Not good. I had to fix it.

"Okay. I'll be right there. Stay where you are." I clicked the phone shut.

"Who is 'her'?" Caldwell asked.

I turned and faced Caldwell. "I didn't tell you everything."

"Where do we need to go to?"

"I can catch a cab."

"Not so easy at this time of night. I can drive you."

"Are you sure?"

"How else am I going to get the full story out of you?"

Once we were in his car, I filled him in. "Dave came to England too."

"So I gathered."

"On the same plane. I saw him. With another woman. Young. Skinny. Her name is Kirstin. Quite a Minnesota name."

"Yes," Caldwell said patiently.

"I was rather angry."

"Mmm."

I couldn't be sure in the dark, but it sounded like his lips had gone rather tight. I wanted to spit the whole story out in one large glob. It felt like it was poison and I had to get it out of my system.

"Well, as I said, they were on the same plane as me. No surprise. Then, almost by accident, I followed them to their hotel. Then, at the bar, I told the blond-haired guy, Guy—remember, the man I was talking to?—about what Dave had done to me. I might have mentioned something about wanting to kill him. Guy was very understanding. Said he knew how I felt. Then the next day I saw Guy talking to Kirstin at the National Gallery. When I tried to catch up to him to see why he was there, he seemed to be giving me a signal."

"A signal?"

"Yeah, the gun-in-the-air signal."

"The gun-in-the-air signal. I'm not familiar with that."

"Yes, you are." I showed him, holding my hand up in the car like it was a gun. "I took it to mean he was on the case. Then he pointed his hand at Kirstin and pretended to shoot her."

"Yow. That doesn't sound good." Caldwell's voice grew thin. "What did you tell him in the bar?"

"That's the puzzling thing. I've tried to remember. I was a bit drunk, but I didn't think I was that bad. I'm not really sure. I've tried to warn Dave that he might be in danger and all that, but I don't think he believed me."

"And now this guy has taken Dave's new girl-friend?"

"It appears. Dave saw them together and she's gone missing. He sounds frantic." I squeezed my hands together. "It's probably nothing, but I'd feel better if we checked it out. Dave's not good in a jam."

"I can't wait to meet him." The dryness in Caldwell's voice would have evaporated a lake.

THIRTY-FOUR

Mosh Pit

I couldn't help it—when I saw Dave I felt sorry for him. He was sitting on a stool scrunched up against the bar. A wall of backs had him fenced in and he was gulping down a pint, wiping at his eyes. I hated to think that he had been crying.

"Karen," he yelled when he saw me and stood, tipping over the stool, sloshing his beer on the coat of a man standing next to him.

Typical Dave, oblivious to the world around him, swaying into the crowd as if entering a mosh pit. At that moment, I couldn't help but see him through Caldwell's eyes, and notice how big and American he seemed. He stood over six feet tall, with a baseball cap over his balding head. He carried his belly proudly under a blue sweatshirt. He was scruffy, with stubble on his face and something red spilled on his chest. I hoped it was ketchup. Had he fought Guy, trying to prevent him from taking Kirstin?

"Do you think he really forced her to go with him? Did you think about calling the police?" I asked.

He shook his head. "I don't know what to do. It was awful. It happened so fast. I just want to find Kirstin." His voice wavered and again I wondered if he was near tears. Give him a plumbing job—no matter how difficult—and he jumped right in, but complications outside that world often frustrated him.

I grabbed for Caldwell's arm and pulled him close to me as we moved closer to the bar and my ex-boyfriend. "Dave, this is Caldwell, the owner of the B and B where I am staying." I thought, *Where we were supposed to have been staying*.

Dave nodded at Caldwell but didn't offer him his hand. "Since he's English, maybe he can talk some sense into this a-hole that grabbed Kirstin."

"Where did you last see her? What happened? Are you sure this guy took her?" I asked.

"It happened so fast. He grabbed her and pulled her away."

"Doesn't make any sense," Caldwell murmured.

Dave lifted a large hand to the top of his head and scratched at his hat as if digging for something important. "Nothing does anymore. I feel completely lost. What did you tell this guy about me? Why is he after us?"

"Let's find Kirstin first. We can talk about that later."

"I'll show you where they went." He walked to the door of the pub and we followed. Caldwell was staring at Dave as if he was some kind of animal he had never seen before.

I whispered to him. "I think he's a little drunk."

"I'd say so," Caldwell said back.

"I'm sorry to drag you into this."

"I feel slightly responsible too. After all, I took you to the pub where you met this Guy fellow."

When we hit the street Dave kept walking. We kept following. As much as I wanted to grab Caldwell's hand, I wasn't sure it was the right time. I had a feeling he was not very happy with me. I guess it didn't look good that I had made so much trouble for my last boyfriend. It would, as the British say, give a person pause for thought.

I caught up with Dave. "Why didn't you stop him from taking her?" I asked.

He kept walking. "It wasn't like that. I didn't have time to think. It all happened in a second. One moment she was standing next to me and the next minute she was gone. All I saw was that he had his arm wrapped around her neck, dragging her off. I couldn't believe it. I ran after them but lost them up by the river. Then I went back to the bar and called you."

"It's a pub," I couldn't help correcting him. "Did he seem dangerous? Did he have a gun or anything?"

"Didn't see one." Dave turned a corner and I saw that we were once again coming up to the Thames. Streetlights shone along the walkway following the river. A few blocks away I could see two people leaning up against a building.

"Is that them?" I asked.

Dave started to trot. I picked up my pace to keep up with him.

Caldwell came abreast of me. "Karen, this is insane. What do you think is going on?"

"I haven't a clue."

All of us slowed down as we got closer to the

couple, trying to see what they were doing. Guy appeared to be grabbing Kirstin by the neck. However, she didn't seem to be struggling.

Dave started to run toward them, yelling, "Let go of her."

Both Caldwell and I stopped.

Yes, Guy had his hands around Kirstin's neck, but he wasn't strangling her—he was kissing her.

And she was kissing him back.

THIRTY-FIVE

Dominoes

Dave squared his shoulders, put his head down, and ran at them. He had been a football player in high school, even if it was thirty-five years ago. Ramming into someone came naturally, I guess.

I should have yelled their names, but I couldn't bring myself to say Kirstin's. Instead I yelled, "Watch out."

Beside me Caldwell murmured, "What's he up to?" while I thought it was fairly obvious.

Dave slammed into the man's back, and the man

went crashing down on top of Kirstin. They toppled like dominoes.

Caldwell and I ran forward to help them all to their feet, but before we could reach them, Kirstin had scrambled out from under, and Dave and Guy—for it was Guy, I could make out his face— were rolling over and over on the ground, trying to clobber each other. Caldwell stepped in closer, maybe thinking of getting between them, and got smacked in the cheek by a backswing from Dave. Kirstin and I both stepped back out of the way.

"Stop them," Kirstin yelled. Then she looked at me and asked, "What are *you* doing here?"

I didn't think I had to answer that question right yet. We watched as Dave straddled Guy, screaming in his face about wanting to kill him. But at least they weren't hitting each other any longer. Caldwell grabbed Dave's shoulder and tried to pull him off. Dave flailed back with his left arm and knocked Caldwell aside.

I turned to Kirstin and asked, "What is going on? What are you doing with Guy?"

"What did you tell him?"

"Long story."

Guy wrapped his legs around Dave and flipped him over, then jumped on top of Dave and pinned his shoulders down.

"When I stepped out of our hotel one night to have a cigarette, Guy came walking by and then we started talking," Kirstin said.

"He picked you up?"

"You could say that. He kept turning up wherever we were."

"It's all my fault. I guess I sicced him on you."

"No way."

Even though I hated it when kids said it, I had to respond, "Way."

Caldwell was making another effort to break up the fight. He grabbed Guy's arm and tried to pull him backward. Guy tipped back and wrapped his arms around Caldwell's neck and tossed him on top of Dave.

Guy was throwing punches at the both of them, Dave was shouting and striking wildly back, and Caldwell was covering his head and kicking.

It was time to step in. I took the only weapon that was close at hand, a book that I had stuffed in my purse when one of the bags was too full, walked up behind Guy and slammed it down on top of his head.

Everything stopped.

Guy toppled backward and sprawled on the ground. Dave sat up with his mouth hanging open, breathing hard. I must have been on a roll, because I lifted the book and hit him on the head.

288 Mary Lou Kirwin

Caldwell sprang to his feet and rushed me, saying, "Well done, my wonderful librarian."

I could tell Caldwell wanted to throw his arms around me, but he stopped a foot or so away. Maybe he was worried I would hit him with the book too. It was all quite confusing.

Kirstin knelt down by Guy and pulled his head into her lap. "Guy? Are you okay?" She glared at me.

I looked at the book in my hands, glad to see it didn't appear to have sustained any damage.

Dave staggered to his feet, holding his head, and swayed over to Kirstin. "What the hell is going on here? Who is this guy and why was he kissing you?"

Guy groaned and sat up. Kirstin helped him, keeping a hand on each shoulder. After a moment, he shook himself and stood up. He reached into his pocket and pulled out a badge. "I'm Inspector Guy Wilkins of the Metropolitan. And you're all under arrest!"

Dave sagged against the railing. "You're a cop? What are you doing with my girlfriend?"

"Your ex-girlfriend! Your previous ex-girlfriend"—Guy looked at me—"told me how awfully you treat your women. I just happened to live right by your hotel, and when I saw Kirstin there one day, I realized who this lovely tall blonde was and started chatting her up. I could tell that she wasn't having the best time. One thing led to another and she has decided that I might be able to show her London in a better light." Guy smiled and wrapped an arm possessively around Kirstin's shoulder. "To put it bluntly, mate, you're just too bloody old for her."

Kirstin leaned her head on Guy's shoulder. I had to admit they made a handsome couple. She looked at Dave and said, "I'll come and get my stuff tomorrow. I'm going home with him."

They started walking away.

"I thought we were under arrest!" Dave shouted after them.

Guy and Kirstin stopped and looked back at us.

"Now you've done it," Caldwell muttered.

Guy shook his head. "Bloody Americans—not worth the paperwork!"

They turned as a unit and walked off down the street.

Dave hung over the railing, staring down into the Thames, and I was afraid he was thinking either of jumping in or throwing up. Caldwell must have had the same thought for he moved a little closer to him.

"Dave," I said. "I'm sorry."

He hung his head and shook it like a dog. "Doesn't matter. Kirstin was boring once the cuteness wore off. I'm glad she's gone. Being with her made me realize how much I missed you. Karen, I'm sorry. I don't know what got into me. I really messed things up."

I couldn't believe what I was hearing. Dave was actually apologizing to me. This was a first.

"Well, I certainly didn't mean for all this to happen," I said.

"But did you have to tell a cop?"

"Well, I didn't know that's what he was. In fact, I thought he was quite the opposite—a dangerous criminal type. Plus, I was pretty drunk when I met him. I'm sure he guessed that."

"You were drunk?" Dave asked.

"The beer is stronger over here."

"You got that right." Dave smiled at me. "I would have liked to see that. Karen the librarian, drunk."

He took a step toward me. "Let's forget this ever happened." He dusted off his sweatshirt. "This whole stinky mess. We've got a couple days left on our vacation. Get your bags and join me. Like this never happened. I'll make it up to you. All of it. I'll do whatever you want to do. We can go to every bookstore in London."

I stood very still, looking past Dave to the Thames. I could feel Caldwell watching me. Dave took another step closer. I thought of a fluffy white mattress floating down the river.

While I no longer wanted to kill Dave—and that

felt very good—neither did I want to spend any more time in his company. I wanted to be with a man who loved books, and loved me loving books.

"I already threw the mattress away."

A laugh barked out of Caldwell. "Karen," he said.

I ran to him and stepped into his arms. The kiss that he gave me made up for absolutely everything bad in my whole entire life. And then some.

THIRTY-SIX

❧

Double Decked

When Caldwell and I came up for air, we were all alone, standing on a lamplit street by the Thames.

He ran his fingers over my cheeks and said, "Sweet one, as I said before, let's go home."

"It's sounding better and better."

We strolled back toward the car, which we had parked in front of the pub. Caldwell linked his arm through mine and I thought of photographs of European couples walking like this, joined so tightly together there was no distance between their bodies as they moved.

Caldwell delivered me to my side of the car and, as he was opening the door, we both looked over and saw Dave standing across the street from the Holiday Inn.

He swayed slightly. His shoulders sagged like two sloppy bags of grain. I couldn't help but feel sorry for him.

"Poor bloke," Caldwell said.

"Yeah, he is."

"He's left with nothing."

"He's got his toilet," I pointed out.

As we stood there watching, Dave glanced the wrong way, then stepped off the curb into the path of a red double-decker bus.

I'm sure he never knew what hit him.

❧

THIRTY-SEVEN

Shelving and Drowning

Shelving books in the Sunshine Valley Library usually soothed my nerves. The task was so methodical and satisfying. Along the way, I would realphabetize the books that had gone astray. Creating order out of a muddle. How nice that there was a certain place, one place only, that a book should be in a library, and I was able to put it there.

While I had returned from England nearly a month ago, I had only been back at work for a couple weeks. As Rosie had warned, the pile on my desk was overwhelming. But everyone had been very kind to me.

Rosie stayed late two nights in a row to help me dig out from under. She even forgave me for calling her in the middle of the night. But then, Rosie was in a very good mood these days.

Today she had another date with Richard.

"You don't mind, do you?" she asked as she pulled on her coat. "That I'm leaving early?"

"No. Can't wait to meet him again." I smiled at her, which made my cheeks feel tight and bulgy. She seemed not to notice how much work it was for me to put on a good face.

I watched her demeanor transform as Richard walked in the door. She blossomed like a flower.

Richard was roughly a foot taller than Rosie, but they probably weighed about the same. When he stood in front of her, he tapped her on the nose. She giggled. They were made for each other.

He nodded at me when we were introduced, but I could see he only had eyes for her. He called her "Bud." Rosie had explained to me that it was short for Rosebud, his nickname for her. "He's into old movies," she had told me. As they left the library they didn't hold hands, but bumped each other gently as they moved along, like cows walking sociably through a pasture.

I was happy for her, but seeing them together really made me feel like crawling onto a shelf and hiding. While I loved my work, I had tasted another life and I had liked it better.

The night that Dave had been killed by the bus was a blur, but a blur that I couldn't see around. I had been put in charge of his body and made responsible for bringing it back to the States. Kirstin had showed up for a moment at his hotel room to get her bags, but afterward had disappeared for good.

Caldwell stood by me the whole time, but we had barely touched after our one big kiss. I just couldn't. He seemed to respect that.

Dave's death was all my fault. I had wanted him dead, I had wished him dead, and this wish had been granted. Now I had to live with it.

Because of me, Guy had met Kirstin. Because of me, Kirstin had left Dave. Then Dave had been so distracted he'd stepped into the path of a bus. Clearly, this, too, was all my fault.

There was a place for everything, and Dave's death landed right plop on my doorstep.

I left England on the day I had planned to leave. Caldwell drove me to the airport, held me by the shoulders, gave me a gentle, undemanding kiss, and said good-bye. All I wanted to do was hold on tight to him and never let him go, but instead I boarded the plane. I flew back with a couple glasses of wine in me and Dave's body keeping company with my luggage.

Caldwell said he would post all my books to me, but they hadn't arrived yet. I kept waiting every day for them, wanting the small piece of England they would carry.

Once I was home, Caldwell called every few days, but I had little to say to him. He seemed so far away. I told him about the funeral. I told him about helping Dave's brother empty out the apartment. I didn't tell him about crying every day. I tried to be cheerful. I couldn't help wondering what he must think of me, all my lies. He told me how Betty and Barb were getting on with the English penal system. It sounded like they were going to rule it accidental homicide and give them each a two-year sentence, but allow them to do community service. Since that was what their lives were anyway—helping others since they'd retired—it shouldn't be hard on them.

I hoped Caldwell wasn't calling just to be nice.

Hay-on-Wye seemed as if it existed in another sphere, another world that circled a different sun in a universe I would never be able to travel to again. Maybe that sounds a little melodramatic, but when I thought of the afternoon I had spent there, it seemed like a taste of paradise: miles of books, a perfect meal by a cozy fire, a man who understood me to my core and liked what he saw there.

I had fallen in deep love with Caldwell, slowly but surely as I had stayed with him, and had only really come to know it as my chance with him was being pulled away by Dave's death. Instead of me taking revenge on Dave, he had done it to me.

A grayness descended upon me. It was only late September in Minnesota, but the days had already turned cold and dreary. The leaves fell without blooming into their usual fall colors.

And as if all of that wasn't bad enough, two nights ago I'd managed to make things even worse.

I had had a few glasses of wine after dinner and decided to send Caldwell an e-mail. I should have known better; certainly the last time I did something spur-of-the-moment after a bit too much to drink, bad things had ensued. But I had only planned on sending him a short note.

However, when I sat down in front of the computer and placed my fingers on the keyboard, words poured out of me:

> I miss you. I miss having breakfast with you. I miss your books and the clean sheets on the bed and the narrow streets of London. Something opened up in me when I was with you and I don't

want it to close again. I feel like I am drowning
without you.

How are you? Do you miss me?

Then I signed it:

Your fellow bookaholic and loving friend, Karen

I sent it.

I hadn't heard from him since. I shuddered when
I thought of what I had done. What had I been
thinking? What if he was never in touch with me
again? How much more could I lose?

The library would only be open for another hour.
I hated to think what I would do at home all by myself. I had thought of taking up knitting, but all I
could think of was Madame LaFarge, who knit as
the world caved in around her. I wasn't quite ready
to step into that role.

As I was putting away the last few books on the
cart, James Patterson mysteries, a writer who had
managed to turn writing into a corporation, I heard
footsteps behind me.

"Excuse me, might you have a copy of the *Pickwick Papers*?" a British male voice asked.

THIRTY-EIGHT

Back Garden, Backyard

I straightened up so fast that I nearly pitched forward. That voice was the dearest thing I had ever heard.

I spun around and there he stood.

Caldwell. Caldwell Perkins himself.

He was dressed as I remembered him—crackling waxed raincoat, tweed sports cap, Scottish wool scarf.

His eyes were as dear and droopy and brown as I remembered them. Two worlds were colliding in front of me, causing atoms of energy to sprinkle the room. How was it possible that he had materialized in front of me, here in the Sunshine Valley Library, in the United States of America?

"You've come," I said, not trying to keep the joy out of my voice.

"I had to bring your books."

"Yes, my books." I dropped the two Pattersons I was carrying.

"You dropped those books," he said, smiling.

"They're not very good books." I stepped over them.

"Have you almost finished work?" he asked.

"I'll get my coat," I said.

I left him standing at the checkout counter and got my coat and purse from my desk. When Nancy looked up, I simply said, "I'm leaving. My friend from England came to get me."

She didn't bother to remind me that I still had an hour left to work.

"How did you get here?" I asked.

Caldwell had a small suitcase and a big box on the floor next to him. "I took a cab."

"You came right from the airport? Why didn't you let me know you were coming?"

He leaned over to lift up the box and said quietly, "I was afraid you might tell me not to."

"How could you think that?"

"Then I got your e-mail and I wanted to surprise you."

"You did. Completely."

We walked to my Toyota and put his luggage in the trunk. Caldwell took off his coat and set it on top of the box. I laughed to see this very British act in Minnesota.

"It's not too cold," he said.

"Not yet," I said.

We got in the car and I started it. I couldn't believe he was sitting next to me. Caldwell was in Minnesota. He had come to see me. I looked over at him. Was this what a prince looked like in middle age?

"Can I take you out to eat?" he asked.

"Not tonight. Let's eat at my house. I can scrounge up something for us. Do you like leftover wild rice hot dish?"

"I've never tried it, but I like the sound of it. Wild rice. What makes it wild?"

"They beat it with paddles to harvest it." I laughed again, this time a nervous laugh, because I didn't know what to do with my hands; they just wanted to touch him. I wrapped them around the steering wheel and pushed on the gas. The car leaped forward down the street.

"Nice library," Caldwell said.

"Yes, it's one of the smaller ones, but cozy."

"How long have you been there?"

"Years and years. The library is also one of the oldest. We even have a copy of the *Oxford English Dictionary* from the twenties, and I love those volumes so. I've told the staff that if there is ever a fire, they should each grab one on their way out the door."

"My, I'd love an old set like that."

My house was only 4.2 miles away from the library. As we drove along, I pointed out the Sunshine Valley water tower, the post office, Gearty Park, which was only a block from my house.

"In the winter, they make a rink and flood it and the kids play hockey," I told him, pointing out the spot. "I can sit at my dining room table and watch them skate around in the dark."

"Hockey? Do you skate?"

"Yes, but not very well. My ankles are weak. I have an old pair of skates."

"Lovely," he said.

"This is my house." I parked in the driveway of my two-bedroom bungalow.

"Very nice. An entire house."

"It's not very big."

"It's practically a manor," he teased.

I went around and opened the trunk.

"Should I bring my things in?" he asked.

"I think you had better."

I grabbed the mail by the front door and let Caldwell into my house, glad that I had straightened it the night before—all the newspapers in the recycling, the dishes clean in the dishwasher.

"What a great house," he said as he walked to my picture window and looked out over my flower garden.

"That's my backyard," I said. "With my flower garden. But I grow no foxglove so you needn't worry."

"Yes," he said. "So this is what a backyard looks like. Very similar to a back garden."

While I reheated the casserole and opened a bottle of red wine, he wandered around looking at my bookshelves, clucking and nodding as he went. Occasionally he'd pull out a book and cluck his tongue.

"You are an Anglophile, aren't you?" he asked.

"Yup."

"You sound more American than I remember."

"Is that good or bad?"

"Neither, just interesting. You must be a bit of a chameleon—blending in wherever you are."

I poured us each a glass of wine and we sat down next to each other on my leather couch in the living room. We clinked glasses.

I said, "I can't believe you're here."

At the same time he said, "I can't believe I'm here. By the way, Twad and Tweed send their love."

"Your cricket buddies. The ones who got me drunk my first night in London. Please give them my regards."

We laughed nervously, then Caldwell grew serious and asked, "How are you, Karen?"

I thought for a moment, determined to try to explain clearly how I was, hoping he would understand. "I feel unreal. I can't seem to be here, back home, but I know I'm not in England. It's like I'm nowhere."

"Yes, I know."

"I can hardly think about what took place on my trip. When I went to England I was so angry with Dave, but I never really wanted anything bad to happen to him. Then I get back home and have to bury him. A few days later, I find out that he did leave me the royalties from the Flush Budget, like he said he would. Don't you see? He wasn't a total bad guy. It's all my fault that he died."

Caldwell carefully set his wineglass down and said in a very controlled manner, "You have got to stop."

"But Dave would be alive if it weren't—"

"That's not the truth. Let me make it clear for you. He left you. He took Kirstin to London. He wouldn't listen to you when you tried to warn him. He lost Kirstin to another man. And he walked in front of a bus—all by himself. Americans do that all the time in London—the left-right thing, you know. You didn't leave him. You didn't go off with another man. Yes, you got angry and let off steam about him to someone else, and that someone else just happened to be a policeman. Who, by the way, knew you were just letting off steam. And who stole the girl away when he got the chance. Then you had to cart your ex-boyfriend's body back to the States and bury him. I would say you got the bad end of the bargain."

"But I'm still alive."

He reached out his hand and touched my shoulder. I could feel his hand through my blouse. A spot of warmth.

"I noticed," he said.

The kitchen timer went off and I jumped up to get the casserole. "I'll bring the food right in. You must be hungry after your long flight and all."

Caldwell grabbed our wineglasses as I took the casserole out of the microwave. I burned my hand on the dish, then decided to give it a minute to cool off. That was when I noticed a letter on the pile of mail that was addressed in handwriting with the return address: KOHLER PLUMBING.

When I opened it, a check for $107,000 fell out. I stared at the amount in amazement. The money from Kohler Plumbing represented the first six-month royalties for the Flush Budget. I'd had no idea that it would amount to this kind of money.

Caldwell was standing in the doorway. I let the check fall to the floor.

"I can't tell you how glad I am that you are here," I said. "I can't stand not being with you."

He took a step toward me. "I feel the same way."

"I guess I have given you my heart," I said.

He pulled me close. "Karen, my own librarian."

I felt completely at home back in his arms. "I was thinking of starting a bookstore with Dave's money. All I need are the books."

"I just happen to have books galore. Might this *bookshop* be named the Karen Nash and Caldwell Perkins bookshop?"

When I tried to agree, he muffled my words by kissing me.

I finally believed he was there.

It was not too good to be true.